I0610950

DANNY AND RON ORLIS

IN THE

SACRED CAVE

DANNY AND RON ORLIS
IN THE
SACRED CAVE

BERNARD PALMER

Please note that several books in the Danny Orlis series are published by Sword of the Lord Publications and are available for purchase on their website, www.swordbooks.com.

Danny and Ron Orlis in the Sacred Cave
© 2023 by Bernard Palmer
All rights reserved. First edition 1956.
Second edition 2023.

Please do not reproduce, store in a retrieval system, or transmit in any form or by any means – electronic, mechanical, photocopying, recording, or otherwise, without written permission from the publisher.

Scripture quotations from The Authorized (King James) Version. Rights in the Authorized Version in the United Kingdom are vested in the Crown. Reproduced by permission of the Crown's patentee, Cambridge University Press.

Cover image: Adobe Firefly

Character illustrations: John Ball

Editors: Jon D. Fogdall, Ruth Clark

Aneko Press Youth

www.anekopress.com

Aneko Press, Life Sentence Publishing, and our logos are trademarks of Life Sentence Publishing, Inc.
203 E. Birch Street
P.O. Box 652
Abbotsford, WI 54405

JUVENILE FICTION / Religious / Christian / Action & Adventure

Paperback ISBN: 978-1-62245-968-1

eBook ISBN: 978-1-62245-969-8

10   9   8   7   6   5   4   3   2

Available where books are sold

CONTENTS

CHAPTER 1

CHANGED PLANS

It was June and dawn came early in the north country. But the birds were up to herald its coming. The early morning breezes were still whispering soft lullabies from the treetops.

Ronald Orlis turned over on his back and stretched luxuriously. He hadn't slept very well that night. He never did the first few nights at home after being away at school. There were too many things to think about. Too many old familiar sounds to hear. Too many things to dream of doing. He closed his eyes again and lay there, listening quietly.

A wild canary had joined the symphony from a perch just outside his window, to trill a triumphant obbligato to the overture. He picked out the shrill voices, one by one, clear and sparkling as the morning sunlight that was shedding its warmth on the little clearing.

He didn't need to get up to know that the mallards nesting in nearby Angle Bay would be circling overhead by twos, on their way to feed. And the ospreys, glistening white against the deep clear blue of the sky, would be soaring, almost motionless, over the still lake. The terns would be hovering greedily over the commercial fishermen's nets for a glimpse of an unsuspecting minnow.

It was good to be home, Ron thought. It seemed better this time than it had ever seemed before. For a long while he soaked in the happy, lilting sounds of the waking day, letting memory fill in the action he knew was taking place. He sighed deeply. It was always good to be home—and hard to leave.

Then Ron heard the *Vigilante's* engine begin to throb. He opened one eye speculatively. Six-fifteen. He might have known. It would take an earthquake, or worse, to make old Cap late for a minute.

He got up after a time and dressed, just in time to see Cap back his little packet boat away from the dock and head out into the creek.

He paused before the door to Danny's room. His older brother would be in there, sleeping. He had a notion to go in and wake him. But that wouldn't do any good, he said to himself. If he was awake, he'd just be waiting until Kay got up so the two of them could go off somewhere together.

That was the trouble with girls, he told himself as he tiptoed down the stairs and out to the dock. Even nice girls like Kay. Let one of them get her hooks into a guy and that was the end of him. He wouldn't even take time to go fishing with his own brother.

* * *

Aunt Mabel had flown up to Cedarton two days before. The public school had been out a week earlier, and Ron and Roxie had already gone home. But she had to wait while Danny and Kay finished their exams before they could join her on the trip up to the Angle.

"I had to leave Mexico and re-enter on a new visa," she had explained, "so I thought I'd come up here and see you, Kay."

"We can go back together"; the girl was thrilled. "Now I won't have to travel alone."

"It's going to be so good to have a little time together before you have to go back to Mexico," Danny had told Kay as they sat on the deck, warming lazily in the gentle June sun.

She nodded.

She looked prettier than ever as she leaned back in the deck chair and closed her blue eyes. Her soft, golden hair had escaped from the silken headscarf and was blowing in wisps about her delicately tanned cheeks, and her lips were parted slightly in a smile that revealed the whiteness of her teeth.

"It's going to be a long three months."

She opened her eyes and looked at him. "But we'll have nine whole months together."

"I know." His voice was distant and far away. "You know, I still keep thinking of Marilyn and what transverse myelitis has done to her body."

"That was God's will for her," Kay had said softly. "We can't understand just why, but it must have been. Otherwise, He surely would have restored her to health with all the prayer that was made."

Danny nodded.

"Marilyn and Chuck surely showed me some things about faith," he said. "They're closer to the Lord now than ever before."

"And happier, too, even though she is in a wheelchair."

Danny thought about all of that as they walked up the path to the cabin. Ron came downstairs to meet him.

"Say, Danny, how about you and me going fishing this morning?" he asked. "The walleyes have been going crazy around Little McCoy."

The young man shook his head. "Kay and I are going out after a while."

Ron's face clouded. "The boat's big enough for three of us, isn't it?" he asked.

"Today it isn't."

"I could run the motor for you."

"Not a chance, Buster."

"I'll put cotton in my ears and close my eyes."

Danny felt the color creep up into his cheeks.

"You can just forget I'm there. I'll even forget it," Ron insisted.

"That won't be hard to do," Danny retorted. "You won't be there."

"Aw, Danny, have a heart."

Kay, who had come into the living room, laughed happily.

"Let him go along, Danny," she said. "I don't mind."

"Nothing doing."

When they had finished breakfast and devotions, Danny went out to get the boat ready while Kay helped Mrs. Orlis with the dishes. It was almost nine o'clock when the two of them got into the boat and shoved away from shore. Danny headed toward Little McCoy, opening the throttle until the broad-beamed boat began to plane.

Neither of them spoke until they reached the west tip of the island and Danny cut the motor to trolling speed, throwing his lure into the water as he did so.

They had only trolled a hundred yards or so when they heard the high-pitched whine of another motor coming across the bay.

"Here come some more fishermen," Kay said.

Danny looked up, scowling.

"I know who that is," he muttered darkly.

Two or three minutes later the other boat slowed to a stop beside them. Ron and Roxie were sitting in it, grinning broadly.

"What's the big idea?" Danny demanded.

"You forgot this," Ron said.

Roxie giggled as her twin held up a second stringer.

"The way the walleyes are biting you'll have to have two stringers. You'll never be able to get them all on one! That is if you do any fishing!"

"Just wait until I get you on shore!"

When they were gone Danny and Kay burst into laughter.

They were still laughing when they had finished fishing and pulled into the Orlis dock about noon.

"I didn't see Tex's plane come in," Danny said, noticing the little floatplane tied in front of one of the tourist's cabins. "Must be something mighty special that brought him out here today. He usually comes on Monday."

In the Orlis cabin Danny's folks, Aunt Mabel, and Tex were all sitting around the dining table. Ron and Roxie were on the old fashioned sofa.

"Well, where's all your fish, big boy?" Danny demanded, rumpling his younger brother's hair. "We got our limit."

Ron looked up at him but did not speak.

"What's the trouble?" Danny asked, staring at first one somber face and then another. "What's wrong?"

"Nothing very much," Aunt Mabel answered. "It's just that I've got to go back to Mexico right away."

Danny Orlis blinked hard.

"But I thought you were going to stay for a week or two," he said.

"So did I." She smiled a little wistfully as she held up a letter. "This came to Tex this morning. It's from the mission board in New York. They sent it to me in care of him, and then wired him, asking him to bring it out at once, so it wouldn't have to wait for the regular mail."

Kay's face was ashen, and her hands were trembling. "Is something wrong at home?"

Aunt Mabel turned to her. "There has been some trouble at our station. Your mother is all right, but the board decided to send in two young men to help the Nelsons, so they're transferring us."

Kay pulled up a chair and dropped into it, weakly. "Are-are you sure Mother isn't hurt?" she asked.

Aunt Mabel laid her work-worn hand on the girl's arm. "Listen to this," she said, opening the letter. "By God's grace Chris wasn't hurt. She wants to stay at El Diablo, but we have two men ready who have volunteered to take that station. For that reason, we are transferring you and Chris to Zongolica."

"Where's that?" Danny broke in.

"Almost down to Guatemala," Ron said. "We just looked it up on a map."

"The change wasn't prompted by the incident at El Diablo alone," Mabel continued to read. "You know we had completed the translation of the Bible into the dialect of the Indians on Superstition Mountain.

However, the translation work at Zongolica is only beginning. Chris will be ready to move next Monday. You should be there by that time if at all possible. Would strongly suggest that you fly."

Danny looked up at Kay.

"That means you'll have to leave first thing in the morning," he said.

Aunt Mabel shook her head.

"Tex wants to fly us down to Minneapolis this afternoon," she said.

CHAPTER 2

UNEXPECTED THINGS HAPPEN

For the space of a minute, silence hung over the room like an early morning fog over Angle Bay. Then Aunt Mabel smiled.

"It looks as though we're going to have to get busy. We'll have to scurry, Kay, if we're going to make the night plane from Minneapolis to Dallas."

Kay got to her feet. She looked at Danny wordlessly. "It's a good thing I'm packed," she managed to say. "I should be ready in half an hour."

Mrs. Orlis looked up at her. "Aren't you going to stay with us?"

Kay shook her head.

"Mother needs me. And besides, I want to do what I can to help. You know, I'm a missionary to Mexico too."

Danny's gaze caught hers and held it for an instant, expressively, saying all the things he wanted to say and couldn't because of the others.

"I'll send you my new address," she told him softly as he carried her suitcase out to the plane, "just as soon as I get it." He grinned crookedly.

He took her hand and held it momentarily before she turned and got into the plane.

"Take care of yourself," he called above the roar of the motor. And then they were gone. Ron came over and stood beside Danny as Tex taxied out to the bay and headed into the wind. A moment later he was airborne, lifting gracefully above the green of the oak and poplar which covered the Canadian shore, and headed toward Baudette.

"I certainly wish they hadn't had to go so soon," Ron observed. "Kay is a swell girl."

Danny looked at him. "You can say that again."

"She's going to make a swell sister."

Danny colored noticeably and took a half-hearted swing at his younger brother.

"Another crack like that and I'll throw you in the lake."

Ron ducked away, laughing.

It was quiet around the house the rest of the afternoon. Ron helped his dad and Danny weed the garden and caulked one of the fishing boats so it wouldn't leak. His older brother worked beside him silently.

"Would you go fishing with me, Danny?" he said at last.

"Sure thing."

Trolling along the south side of Little McCoy Island, Ron leaned back against the motor, lazily.

"It would certainly be something to get to go down to Mexico, wouldn't it?" he asked.

"I don't know," Danny answered. "Things were pretty hot when Jim and I were there two years ago. It might not be as much fun as you think."

"Now don't tell me you wouldn't jump at a chance to get down there this summer, Danny," Ron laughed.

He caught a fish just then and Danny used the dip net silently.

Saturday and Sunday passed slowly. On Monday morning the boys planned on going fishing again, but they waited until after the mail boat came in.

"Do you think you'll get a letter from Kay?" Ron asked with mock sincerity. "Do you suppose she wrote a letter to you an hour after they left here and mailed it in Minneapolis?"

"I'd never tell you if she did."

There was no letter from Kay, but there was a letter in a long envelope from Cedarton. Danny put it aside while he helped his dad with the outgoing mail, and it wasn't until he went to lock the post office that Ron remembered it.

"What about that letter of yours, Danny?" he asked.

"I suppose it's from one of the fellows who's going to summer school." He took the envelope and ripped it open.

Ron moved behind him and tried to peer over his shoulder.

"Get out of here!" He turned away from his younger brother. "Why, it's from Mr. Forester," he said a moment later.

"What does he want?"

"Just listen to this." Danny's voice was trembling as he read. "It's taken me quite a while to get the arrangements made, but I just finished them this afternoon. I bought a station wagon for your Aunt Mabel and Kay's mother to use at their new station in Mexico."

"A station wagon!" Ron exclaimed. "What a gift!"

"I wrote to you," Danny read on, "because I knew there was no way of contacting Mabel or Kay by phone. Tell them to phone me when they are ready to leave Warroad or Baudette and I'll have it ready, so they won't have to wait for it."

"But they've already gone," Ron moaned. "They're in Mexico by this time."

Mr. Orlis pursed his lips thoughtfully as he read the letter. "I think you had better go into town on the mail boat, Danny, and call Mr. Forester. He can probably make arrangements for the station wagon to be shipped to Mexico City."

In Warroad Danny and Ron put in a call to Mr. Forester and told him what had happened.

There was a long silence.

"I know you're needed at the Angle, Danny," he said at last. "But I can't get away from here for another six months, and the women could get a great deal of good out of the station wagon by that time. Do you think you and Ron could take it down there? I'll pay your expenses."

The older boy hung up slowly.

"Did he want us to take that station wagon down to Mexico, Danny?" Ron asked, his voice tinged with excitement.

"Did you ever hear such a crazy idea?"

"It doesn't sound crazy to me," Ron retorted. "It sounds wonderful."

Carl Orlis pulled at the lobe of his ear, thoughtfully. "They do need that station wagon," he said. "Mabel was telling me just before she left that there were a few pretty good roads down in the area where they're going. She said that some of the people have used a vehicle with four-wheel drive very successfully. It would be a big help."

"I don't know," Danny said doubtfully. "I'd certainly like to go, but I'm going to have some stiff bills to meet if I'm going to stay in school next year. I've been counting on what I could make as a guide this summer to get me through the next term."

His mother smiled confidently.

"We have a wonderful God, Danny."

Roxie's lips quivered. "Do you mean they're going to get to go and I'm going to have to stay at home?" she asked.

Mrs. Orlis put her arm about her tenderly. "There are times when we all have to make sacrifices," she said.

It took almost a week for Mr. Forester to get the station wagon properly equipped. He put the newest all terrain tires all around, and had special mattresses made so that it could be used for sleeping, if necessary. The evening Ron and Danny came into Cedarton on the bus. The last of the work was done, and the car was washed, greased, and ready for the long trip south.

Mr. Forester met them at the bus depot. He spoke to them warmly enough but seemed strangely preoccupied as they drove along. Finally, he pulled over to the curb and stopped.

"I've got something I'd like to talk with you about," he said, "before I get to the house where Carrie and Marilyn might happen to overhear us."

There was something mysterious about his manner that caused Ron's heart to stir. The boy looked about in the growing dusk, as though he expected to see someone lurking in the shadows spying on them.

"I have a good friend who's very high in the Mexican government," Mr. Forester continued, involuntarily lowering his voice. "I wrote to him for information about bringing the station wagon into the country and he asked me to perform a very important service for him."

Ron's mouth dropped open, and his eyes widened.

"The man is a Christian and is doing a great piece of work for the Lord. I hesitated to have the women missionaries do it for him, but if you fellows are willing to run the risk, I'd certainly like to help him."

"What does he want us to do?"

"He's got some equipment up here to use in archaeological exploration. He wanted me to get it delivered to him."

"What sort of equipment?" Ron blurted.

"Oh, the usual thing, spades, picks, shovels, ropes, and so on. I've got a list of them."

The boys both looked at Mr. Forester strangely. "But why be so secretive about that?" Danny asked. "And why send way up here to get it? He should be able to get that sort of thing right in Mexico City."

"That's what I thought, too," Mr. Forester answered, "but he seemed so insistent. And he's an honorable man. I know he was telling the truth when he said that it was both important and dangerous."

Danny looked at his younger brother. "What do you say?" he asked. "We're both in this thing together."

"It's all right with me," Ron said doubtfully. "But I don't know what there is that's so dangerous about a shovel unless a guy is allergic to work."

"Fine," Mr. Forester answered. "I was sure we could count on you."

When they walked up the steps to the Forester home, Marilyn came out into the living room in her wheelchair.

"Danny and Ron!" she exclaimed happily. "It's so good to see you."

"How are things going?" Danny asked her, marveling at the sparkle in her eyes.

"They couldn't be better," she said, her voice ringing.

That evening when they were all in the living room Marilyn turned to her father.

"Dad," she said abruptly, "I've just thought of something. You know how concerned we've been over Newton Bostwick, about his soul, I mean."

Her father nodded.

Marilyn turned to Danny and Ron. "Newton is Mother's nephew," she said, and then turned to her father again.

"Only last night you were saying that if he could spend some time with Ron and Danny, it might help him a lot." She paused for a moment. "Do you suppose it would be possible for him to go along?"

Mr. Forester's eyes lit up. "That's a great idea, Marilyn. I'll call his folks right now." He turned to the boys, "if it's all right with Danny and Ron."

CHAPTER 3

A THIRD PASSENGER

Early the next morning Ron and Danny packed their clothes and camping equipment in the station wagon while Mr. Forester boxed the supplies his Mexican friend asked him to send down to Zongolica.

"Now remember, you're to stop on the American side of customs to have the car greased and serviced. And whatever you do," he cautioned them as they crawled into the vehicle and Danny started the motor, "don't say anything to anyone about the boxes, or archaeology, or anything remotely connected with the subject."

Ron shook his head. "I certainly don't get it, but you can count on us to keep our mouths shut. We don't want to get mixed up in anybody else's trouble, especially when it doesn't make sense to us."

They drove up to a large house in Minneapolis and a pudgy, round-faced boy about Ron's age, with a mop of curly red hair and a fistful of freckles scattered across the bridge of his nose, came out with his suitcase.

"I thought you guys were going to be here two hours ago," he grumbled, throwing his bag into the back.

Ron got out to let him in, but he shook his head. "I always ride next to the window," he announced. "I don't like to sit in the middle." Ron looked at him strangely and started to speak but stopped with the words dangling on the very tip of his tongue.

"Okay, Red. I'm like Kay, I enjoy sitting next to Danny."

The other boy bristled. "My name isn't Red," he informed Ron. "I'll thank you to refrain from calling me that."

"Sure, Red," the younger Orlis boy grinned. "Anything you say."

The newcomer drew himself up haughtily. "My name," he said grimly, "is Newton Jonathan Edward Bostwick III."

Danny glared at Ron in warning, but it was no use. That look had come into his eyes again.

"I know," he said seriously, "I could call you, Third." He tried it, rolling the word off his tongue with great relish while Newton's face flushed as red as his hair. "Third. Third. Nope, that would never do. People would just think I lisped. But I'll think of something, Red, old boy. Don't you worry about it."

Newton snorted to himself and squeezed over

against the door until a narrow space of leather showed on the seat between him and Ron.

"I'm sure this is going to be a very enjoyable trip," Newton said to no one in particular, his lips curling about the words.

"You'd better take it easy, Ron," Danny muttered softly.

That first night when it came time to sleep, they pulled over to the side of the road and stopped. Ron got his sleeping bag from the back of the station wagon.

"I'll tell you what," he said, looking at Danny and winking. "I'll sleep in this thing tonight. Then when we get down where there are rattlesnakes and Gila monsters, you guys can sleep in it."

"For your information," Newton told him, "my uncle bought this station wagon and paid for it. He said that I could sleep in it every night if I wanted."

The Orlis boys looked at one another and smiled.

That night they ate around an open campfire, and when they finished, Ron went back to the station wagon and got his Bible.

"Why don't we have our devotions out here, Danny?" he asked. "There's something about reading the Bible out in the open that really tops off the day for a fellow."

The older boy took the Bible and opened it thoughtfully.

"The Bible?" Newton echoed. "You don't mean to

tell me that you actually believe the Bible, and read it?" He laughed sarcastically.

"It's the Word of God," Ron countered. "Of course, we read it."

Newton laughed again. "I can see reading it for laughs, but you certainly aren't naive enough to believe that assortment of wild tales and legends, are you? Why, I put those in their proper place when I was ten years old."

"So did I," Danny answered. "I was just ten when I confessed my sin and put my trust in the Lord Jesus."

A peculiar, superior-looking grin twisted Newton's round face. He shook his head. "I feel sorry for both of you. I actually do."

"You can save your sorrow for yourself, Newton," Ron told him gently. "We have taken Christ as our Savior. We know where we are going to spend eternity."

For an instant, the mockery went out of the other boy's face.

"I can't figure him out, Danny," Ron said when the two of them were alone together for the first time, the third day after leaving Cedarton. "He acts like such a dope, but he uses words a mile long."

"Didn't I tell you?" Danny laughed. "He's something of a genius or a child prodigy. He's only fourteen, the same as you are, but he's exceptionally bright."

Ron's forehead wrinkled uncertainly. "You can tell that he's a brain all right; but if he's so smart, why does he feel like he does toward the Bible?"

"The only way I can understand that is by turning to the Scriptures. You know we're told that some of the wisest and most intelligent will turn away, and sometimes the simplest will accept Him." Danny paused for a moment. "I'm glad we don't have to be so smart and intelligent to understand spiritual things. They're so simple even a child can understand them."

Ron turned and looked up the street to see Newton Jonathan Edward Bostwick III come swaggering toward them.

"Red's simple, too, Danny, in an intelligent sort of way."

The forest had disappeared as they went south. The cornfields came and went, and at last they were in the stifling hot cattle country of Texas.

"What I would like to know," Newton said for the fourth time that morning, "is what you've got in those heavy wooden crates up on the carrier?"

Ron looked around stealthily, then leaned over to his companion. "There's going to be a revolution in Mexico," he whispered, "and we're smuggling guns and ammunition to them."

Newton snorted.

"Don't be juvenile."

They were approaching a dirty little town on the Texas border. "How about stopping here to eat?"

"I could go for a good steak," Newton announced.

"Steak?" Ron echoed.

"Steak, my eye," his older brother said. "We'll be lucky to get hamburgers."

They sat down at a little table in one corner of the cafe and picked up the menu. A short, moon-faced character with a long scar on his upper lip came out of the kitchen, wiping his hands on a grimy rag.

"Does that station wagon out there belong to you guys?" he asked, motioning carelessly with his thumb.

The Orlis boys nodded.

"As a matter of fact," Newton announced loudly, "we're driving it down to Zongolica, that's in Mexico, you know, for my uncle."

Danny straightened quickly and jabbed the other boy under the table with his foot.

But it was too late. Everyone in the cafe had heard him.

"It's too bad you missed your friend," the waiter went on loudly.

"Friend?" the boys echoed.

"Sure. Didn't you know he was coming?" By this time everyone in the cafe was staring at them. "He was here yesterday, and again this morning. Asked if I'd seen two boys in a blue station wagon. Guess he didn't know there were three of you."

There was a long, heavy silence.

"What did he look like?" Danny asked, scarcely mouthing the words. "This fellow who is supposed to be our friend."

The waiter thought momentarily, pursing his lips. "Well now, let me see. He was a tall feller, with sandy hair and bushy eyebrows, and drove a big black car with Texas license plates. You must be the ones he was looking for. He described you to a tee, except for the fat one there."

Newton Bostwick bristled at that, and Ron managed to choke off a snicker.

The boys finished eating hurriedly and rushed outside.

"I did think we'd stay here for tonight," Danny said when they were alone, "but I believe we'd better go on now. There's no telling what this might mean."

"Don't be naive," Newton told him. "This is not television, you know. You won't find a robber under every bush."

Nevertheless, they drove down to the customs office, stopped to service the car in the station Mr. Forester mentioned, and crossed the border. The officials checked their bags carefully.

Danny was the spokesman for the trio. Newton pushed past Ron rudely, and crowded up to where he could talk with the officer too. As Ron turned to let their companion pass, he chanced to glance back. There behind them stood a tall, swarthy stranger with bushy eyebrows. He had been staring hard at them, but when Ron saw him, he turned quickly away. The young Orlis boy caught his breath sharply.

"I tell you I saw him, Danny," Ron insisted as they drove away from the customs office. "I know it was him. And he was staring at us like everything."

"Are you sure?"

"He had bushy eyebrows, and his car was black and had a Texas license."

"Still playing cops and robbers," Newton observed. "When are you going to grow up, Ronald?"

"When I'm sure that guy's not following us, Red."

The road was smooth and well-marked, and Danny was able to make good time. They passed through a dozen squalid little villages, each with half a handful of adobe huts and the ever-present chickens and pigs. However, there were a couple of up-to-date modern little cities on the highway too, cities that, except for the dark-skinned people and the innumerable donkeys, could have been anywhere in the States.

When evening came, they pulled off the highway and made their beds. It was Danny's turn to sleep outside. He took the sleeping bag up on a little knoll fifty or sixty feet away and crawled into it.

Newton turned his back on Ron deliberately and moved as far away from him as possible. But the young Orlis boy was too tired to care. He closed his eyes and fell asleep almost instantly.

How many hours had passed he did not know, but he stirred restlessly and rubbed his eyes. There was a faint, stealthy sound outside. He moved again. From far off he could hear it, a muffled footstep, tiptoeing over the stony ground. It should mean something to him, but he was so very tired, and sleep was still so near.

It came again! This time just outside the station wagon! Instantly he was awake! He sat up silently. His blood chilled in his veins and his heart skipped erratically. He swallowed hard, as though to keep it in place. Someone was out there!

"Newton!" he whispered softly, punching his chubby companion in the ribs. "Newton!"

The boy groaned in protest and turned over.

There was silence around the station wagon, a tense, expectant silence that seemed about to smother him!

The moon had long since gone and the darkness was that of ebony. He could scarcely see the hood ornament on the station wagon. Whoever was out there was at the back of the vehicle. He heard him again.

"Danny!" Ron shouted at the top of his voice. "Shoot him! He's back here! Shoot him!"

Newton leaped out of bed and scrambled toward the door. "Don't shoot! Don't shoot!" he cried.

Outside the station wagon a hard, metallic object clattered to the stony ground, and there was the sound of footsteps, running. A moment later Danny shouted.

"What happened?" Newton demanded, his voice quavering. "What's wrong? W-w-why did you yell th-th-that way?"

By that time Danny ran up and jerked open the door to the station wagon. "What's the matter, Ron?" he cried.

"He was out here," Ron told them. "I heard him."

"You must be imagining things."

"No, I didn't. I heard him. He dropped something back by the left rear wheel."

Danny took the flashlight from the glove compartment. A minute later he was back.

"Somebody was here, all right," he said. "But I can't tell you what he was doing. Look at these."

His hand was trembling as he thrust a compact pair of wire cutters into the yellow beam of light.

"What could you do around a car with wire cutters?" Ron asked him.

Slowly he shook his head. "There are a good many things about this trip that don't make sense to me."

"I-I'm going back," Newton Jonathan Edward Bostwick III told them, his lips quivering. "I-I'm going to the next town and go back. W-w-why, he could have killed me!"

"With a pair of wire cutters?" Ron wondered.

Newton didn't think he was funny.

CHAPTER 4

THE CHASE BEGINS

Danny Orlis crawled into the station wagon and closed the door. Although they were well into Mexico, the night air in that high altitude was chilly. He switched on the map light and studied the wire cutters carefully, turning them over in his hand.

Newton Bostwick had crawled out of the covers and was leaning over the front seat, looking at Danny plaintively.

"Do-do you think that fellow will come back?" he stammered.

The older Orlis boy shook his head. "The way he ran, I don't think he'll be back here tonight," he said. "But there's no way of knowing."

"I don't m-m-mind telling you," Newton went on weakly, "I-I'm frightened."

"You aren't alone," Ron confessed. "Let's get out of here, Danny, before that joker comes back."

Danny switched on the ignition but hesitated uncertainly. "I don't know whether it's best to move or not. The fellow will expect us to get out of here as quickly as we can. If he's looking for us, he'll probably be looking for us out on the road."

"If we get that far we'll have a chance to outrun him," Ron said earnestly. "I'm going to get out of here if I've got to walk."

"I am, too," Newton added.

"Now you're talking sense, Red."

"Ronald," the other boy informed him crisply, "I much prefer not to be called Red."

"Okay, Red."

Danny Orlis meshed gears and started to back around to drive back the same way they came.

"Did it ever occur to you, Daniel," Newton asked in all seriousness, "that if our assailant is going to ambush us, he will be waiting for us to drive back down the trail we traversed to reach this point of seclusion?"

Ron wrinkled his forehead. "What does he mean, Danny?" he asked. "Did he say that guy'd be waiting for us somewhere along the trail?"

"Precisely," Newton affirmed.

The older Orlis boy turned the thought over in his mind carefully. "That's something I hadn't thought of, Newt, but it does make sense. Thanks."

"Why thank him?" Ron wanted to know. "He's got his neck up here the same as you and me."

"Take it easy, Ron," Danny cautioned. "I'm used to your corny jokes, but I don't think Newt appreciates them."

"I am sorry to have to call your attention to this matter, Daniel," Newton said prudishly, "but I find the nickname 'Newt' extremely distasteful. It is almost as revolting as 'Red.' I much prefer to be called by my given name, Newton."

"Sure thing," the older Orlis lad answered. "I'm sorry if I offended you. I certainly didn't intend to."

"Your apology is accepted."

There was another road which wound across the mountainside, along a steep cliff and around a huge stack of boulders. Finally, it headed down to the main road. As they pulled onto the transcontinental highway all three boys looked about anxiously.

"Well," Ron sighed, "it looks as though we gave them the slip."

"Yes," Danny replied, "thanks to Newton, here."

The red-haired boy drew himself up proudly. "That was rather clever of me, wasn't it? I'm sure you would have blundered, ignorantly, back down that same trail if I hadn't been along to acquaint you with its dangers."

Ron looked at him bewilderedly.

"Oh, brother!" he muttered under his breath.

Danny shifted into high and urged the powerful station wagon up to within a shade of the legal speed limit. Faint gray streaks of dawn were rending the darkness to the east, like the first probing patrols of an advancing army, which in another hour would command the whole countryside, and by midmorning would be blistering every living thing with withering fire.

"We're lucky to have gotten as much sleep as we did," Danny said. "We should be able to drive all day without getting tired."

"Sleep?" Newton echoed, shuddering. "I doubt that I shall ever sleep again."

"Me neither," Ron added, "only I don't say it so elegant like."

"You know," Danny said after a time, "I still can't understand what that fellow was doing at the back of the station wagon with wire clippers. If he'd had a knife, I'd have thought he was going to slash a tire. But what can you do to a car with a pair of wire clippers?"

Ron shrugged his shoulders.

"Search me."

"I should think," Newton observed, his freckled face twisted into a superior little smile, "that it might be the point of wisdom to bring the vehicle to a halt and examine it carefully."

"Bull's eye, Newt!" Danny exclaimed, slowing. "I mean Newton. You've rung the bell again. Is there anything coming, Ron?"

"Just that old guy on his donkey," the younger boy said, "the one we just passed."

Danny braked the car smoothly and stopped on the shoulder of the highway.

"You two get out and look around back there," he ordered. "I'll stay in the car and keep the motor running in case we have to get away in a hurry."

"Don't you go to leaving too fast," Ron cautioned as he crawled out of the station wagon, "if there is something coming. I want to get back in before you take off."

"Don't be absurd," Newton chided.

The two boys went to the back of the station wagon and looked around.

"I see nothing amiss," Newton said.

He started back to the front door, but Ron lay down in the dust and pulled himself under the rear axle.

"I see it, Danny!" he shouted. "There's a copper box wired to the frame."

"What?"

"Get me those wire cutters! There's a box under here!"

As Danny opened the front door to get out, he noticed a car nosing over the hill behind them about a mile away.

"Somebody's coming, Ron! Get in!"

The boy scrambled out from under the station wagon. Newton, his face ashen, had scooted over into the center of the seat. Ron jumped in beside him and they were away in a swirl of dust. The other car was still behind them.

"Did I hear you say there's a box wired under the station wagon?" Danny asked when they had regained speed.

"Precisely," Ron said, looking over at Newton.

"What was it like?"

Newton had turned, and was staring, wide-eyed, at Ron.

"It's a copper box about so big," measuring the air with his hands.

Danny moistened his lips thoughtfully.

"And I found it all by myself," Ron continued. "Rather clever of me, wasn't it?"

Danny choked suddenly.

The boys had forgotten about the car behind them until the horn honked raucously. All three of them jumped! Danny pulled over to let a sleek, black American-made car go by.

"Did you see that chap?" Newton asked, his voice taut. "It's the same tall individual with the protruding eyebrows. The one who stood behind us at the customs office."

"Are you sure?" Ron asked him.

"They tell me I have a photographic mind," Newton informed them. "I never forget a face."

Ron shivered. "That's one I'd like to forget."

If the other driver had any interest in them, he gave no sign. The road was good and fairly straight, and he drew away from them steadily.

"I hope that's the end of him," the young Orlis boy said.

Danny pulled over to the side of the road and stopped.

"Now what?" Newton demanded, forgetting his eight-cylinder vocabulary for a moment.

"We've got a powerful hankering to see what's in that box," Ron told him. As he crawled out of the car he turned to Danny. "Throw me those wire cutters, fella."

"Here, I'll help you."

"Nothing doing. You stay in there with your foot on the gas. We might have to get out of here, pronto!"

Newton sat in the station wagon, quivering like a jellyfish while Ron crawled under the rear axle and cut the box free. In a moment he was back.

"I got it, Danny," he gasped. "Let's get going."

While Danny drove, Ron broke the spots of solder which held the lid closed.

"That wasn't on the car when we left Cedarton," Danny said. "That fellow in the service station near customs must have put it there. But whoever fastened that under there must have been mighty particular to go to all of that trouble."

"Maybe this is what Mr. Forester's Mexican friend wanted us to bring into the country for him," Ron suggested, "instead of all those shovels and picks and ropes."

Newton turned to face him. "Why did you refer to my uncle?" he asked.

"Ron talks too much," Danny answered. "Maybe we'd better not open that box, fellows," he said after a moment or two. "It isn't ours, you know."

But Ron already had the lid loosened.

"We've got to see what's in it, Danny," he went on, "after all the trouble it's caused us."

Before his brother could protest further Ron jerked the lid off the box.

"An old book!" he exclaimed.

"What would my uncle be doing with a thing like that?" Newton asked Danny, almost belligerently.

"Who wrote it?" the older boy queried, ignoring Newton's question.

"How should I know?" Ron asked, scratching his ear. "I could make more sense out of a bunch of squirrel tracks in the snow."

"Must be Spanish."

Newton smiled. "If you must know," he announced, "the writing is neither squirrel tracks nor Spanish. It is Latin."

Ron stared at him admiringly. "We've got a set of encyclopedias at home, only they don't talk."

"Do you think you can read it, Newton?" Danny asked him.

"I had two years of Latin," the freckled-faced boy said, "and learned to converse very well in the language with my instructor. It should be quite simple to read this book—or I should say, manuscript, since it is written with pen and ink."

"Okay," Ron said irritably. "Read."

Newton took the book and, as Danny drove along the highway, he studied the first few pages.

"Something is amiss here, Daniel," he said after ten or fifteen minutes.

"You mean you aren't so smart after all?" Ron asked, almost hopefully.

"I mean," Newton began, sweeping Ron disdainfully with a glance, "that the Latin in this manuscript is badly garbled. The spelling is atrocious, the punctuation is frightful, and the sentence structure does not follow that of classic Latin."

"Outside of that it's pretty good, huh?"

"Ron," Danny said, "take it easy. What do you make of it, Newton? Can you read any of it at all?"

"I might be able to if I could work at it," he said, "but it appears to have been written by a half-educated individual by the name of Don Jose Maria Diego. I would guess that he is using the punctuation and sentence structure of another language."

Danny scratched his head. "I just can't make it out," he said. "Why would anyone want to steal an old book like this, when it isn't even in good Latin?"

"Why would anyone fasten it under our station wagon?"

"And," Newton added, his eyes searching Danny's face, "what does my uncle, Harold Forester, have to do with it?"

While Danny was desperately searching for words, they passed a black car by the side of the road.

"That's him!" he exclaimed, his voice catching a little.

Ron whirled to stare through the rear window.

"He's starting up, Danny! He's going to follow us!"

"W-w-what are we going to do?" Newton asked, his voice breaking suddenly to a hoarse whisper.

"Ron," Danny said, glancing down at the speedometer, "is he gaining on us?"

The younger boy waited a moment, watching. "A little."

The silence in the front seat of the station wagon was heavy.

"Pray, fella," Danny continued at last.

"What good would that do?" Newton murmured.

Ron acted as though he hadn't even heard Newton as he bowed his head.

"Oh, Father God," he began softly, "we know that You have told us to come to You when we are in need, and that You will hear and answer our petitions. Be with us. Keep us safe and help us to carry out the things You would have us do. In Jesus' name. Amen."

When he looked up, he was surprised to see that Newton had bowed his head too.

There was a sudden screech of brakes! The station wagon lurched! Young Orlis was thrown violently against the door!

"What's the matter, Danny?" he cried.

"We got ahead of Bushy Eyebrows far enough to get a couple of blind corners between him and us, so I turned off the road!"

Ron looked at the huge boulders which screened them from the view of the highway. Danny had only seconds to spare. The black sedan went roaring by.

"There," Newton said, breathing deeply, "we have deceived him."

"In English," Ron grinned, "we've given him the slip."

"But only for a few minutes," Danny told them. "We've got to think of something else fast!"

CHAPTER 5

THE GOAL REACHED

"**W**e can't stay here!" Newton blurted. Again, his fancy language slipped from him. "There isn't any place for us to go if he does miss us and comes back right away! We'll be trapped!"

Danny was already backing up.

"I thought of that," he said. "There are some side roads that go over the mountain instead of around it. I noticed them as we drove along. Check the map and pick out one, Ron, while I double back. Be sure to choose one that joins the main highway again."

"I don't like this," Newton muttered. "I don't like it at all."

"Can't say that Danny and I are exactly crazy about it, either," Ron replied. "Take the next road to the left, Danny. It looks like our best choice."

"Fine."

Ron and his red-headed companion kept staring

back, as though they expected Bushy Eyebrows to come back to pounce upon them. Danny slowed the station wagon and turned up the narrow, winding trail toward the top of the mountain, shifting smoothly into second gear.

"I don't know why I ever came along on this ridiculous trip," Newton grumbled as the station wagon toiled slowly up the steep slope.

"It's almost dark," Danny said, noticing for the first time that the sun had sunk beyond the horizon. "Why wouldn't this be a good place to stop for the night?"

"Looks all right to me," Ron put in.

They ate cold sandwiches for supper that evening, not daring to risk a fire, and as soon as they had finished, they made the bed in the back of the station wagon.

"Well," Ron said, grabbing the sleeping bag, "I guess it's my turn to bunk with the rattlesnakes."

Newton, who had been in the back of the station wagon, crawled out.

"It's my turn," he announced, reaching for the bag.

"But I thought—" young Ron protested.

"Even though this station wagon does belong to my uncle, and I have a legitimate claim to sleeping in it, I prefer to assume my portion of the discomforts of this miserable journey." He bit his lower lip to keep it from trembling. "In other words, if anybody is going to sleep with rattlesnakes, I will be the one!"

"Say, Red," Ron exclaimed admiringly, "you're all right!" Newton tucked the sleeping bag beneath his arm clumsily.

"The name," he said, "is Newton."

With that he turned and strode uncertainly away. Ron watched him momentarily as he dropped the sleeping bag to the ground and looked at it in bewilderment, then he walked over to him.

"Here," he said, "let me show you how to fix that. You want to blow up the air mattress first and put it in this pocket on the underside of the bag. And then stake this flap in place to keep the wind off your head."

Newton watched intently while Ron fixed his bed. When at last he had finished, the red-haired boy touched his arm self-consciously.

"Thanks," he managed. "I never did know how you worked one of those things."

By this time darkness had closed in about them. Ron and Newton got back into the car with Danny. The three of them sat for a moment or two in the front seat of the station wagon.

"Wish we could turn on the map light, or a flashlight," Ron said. "We should have our devotions before we turn in."

"We can quote some verses," Danny told him.

He began with verses he had learned years before in the little Sunday school up on the Angle.

Ron continued with verses of assurance and the promise of answered prayer and salvation. Newton had been sitting there, silently. The Orlis boys hadn't even known whether he had been listening. Now he broke in suddenly.

"What does that mean?" he asked. "'By grace are ye saved through faith'?"

Ron paused, groping for words. He looked over to Danny hopefully, but his brother said nothing.

"It means that we must believe in order to have eternal life," Ron answered at last. "We must recognize that we are sinners and need a Savior. Then we must put our trust in the Lord Jesus, and we are Christians, or as that verse says, we are saved."

Newton pursed his lips.

"Wouldn't you like to be a Christian?" Ron asked him.

He took a deep breath. "I can't understand," Newton continued, "how any intelligent person can believe that the assortment of myths and half-truths and errors that make up the Bible can be the Word of God."

Ron turned to his older brother.

"The Bible doesn't need any defense, Newton," Danny began easily. "It was here thousands of years before we were born and, if Christ tarries, it will be here long after we're gone. A ten-year-old science book is hopelessly out of date, yet the Bible, old as it is, is as fresh, new, and true today as it was the very day it was written."

Newton had nothing to say.

Ron talked with him for a while about the Lord,

but he evaded the questions or ignored them. Finally, he got up and started toward his sleeping bag.

"See you in the morning."

When he was gone Ron turned to his brother. "You know something," he said. "Red's got some dopey ways, but he's really all right. He was so scared out there a few minutes ago when I helped him lay out his sleeping bag that I thought he was going to keel over, but he made up his mind he's going to stay out there tonight. And that's what he's doing."

"Pray for him, Ron," Danny said. "He's got a wonderful mind, but he is blind spiritually."

Ron had thought he wouldn't be able to go to sleep at all that night, but after lying for a few minutes looking up toward the top of the station wagon he closed his eyes. The next thing he knew it was morning.

Danny was already awake and cooking breakfast beside a little fire some ten or fifteen feet to one side of the car. Newton was up and had his sleeping bag rolled.

"Hi, Red," Ron sang out. "How'd you and the rattlesnakes get along last night?"

Newton looked at him seriously. "It was quite cozy," he said. "I used the bag for half the night, then they awakened me, and I allowed them to use it."

Ron looked at him quizzically. From anyone else that remark would have been a joke. But how could a fellow tell what a guy like Red meant by what he said?

"I think we've given Bushy Eyebrows the slip, all right," Danny said as they ate.

"That doesn't make me mad," Ron answered. "I only hope that we're rid of him for good."

They finished breakfast hurriedly and Danny drove over the mountain, past a little village, and out onto the highway.

"Now," Ron said triumphantly, "we're on our way to Zongolica."

A scowl came across Newton's face.

"I can't conceive of anything drearier," he said. "I suppose it will be another of these squalid little villages we've been seeing."

"Why, didn't you know?" Ron asked. "They're building a swanky new hotel just for us and covering all the stores and houses with gold leaf."

"Your humor, Ronald," Newton said mirthlessly, "is very droll."

Ron turned to Danny. "Now what did he mean by that?"

It did seem as though they had given the bushy-eyebrowed stranger the slip. They drove all that day and the next without seeing him; through Mexico City and down the Pan-American highway toward the little jungle town of Zongolica.

The country changed as they drove. The mountains gave way to vast stretches of desert where nothing except cacti and thin scrub grasses grew. The desert became mountains again. Palm trees appeared, and then they were in the semitropical jungle. Swamplands, an almost impenetrable tangle of vines and brush and trees, lay on either side of the road. Mountains thrust against the sky as though to hold the blue waters back, and here and there a few haphazard little huts scarred the deep, even sea of jungle green.

Finally, on the afternoon of the third day, they pulled into Zongolica. It wasn't difficult to find the mission headquarters in the little city. Ron got out and asked the first person he met, trying to pronounce the words he had looked up in the Spanish dictionary.

"Who you want?" the Indian asked in fair English.

Ron's mouth sagged open. "Where did you learn to speak English?"

"I work in beet fields many times," the Mexican answered brokenly. "Colorado."

When Ron asked him about the mission station, he pointed up the street to a fairly large, well-painted building.

Kay, Christine, and Aunt Mabel came running out to the porch in answer to Danny's blast of the horn.

"I want to warn you, Red," Ron said under his breath, "Danny's already got Kay spoken for. You won't have a chance of getting her away from him."

Danny grinned a little, in spite of himself, but there was no smile on Newton's face.

"My name is not Red," he snapped, "and I haven't the slightest interest in the opposite sex."

"Me neither," Ron said, "or maybe I should say they don't have any interest in me."

By that time Kay had run around the station wagon to Danny's side.

"Oh, Danny!" she gasped softly.

"Surprised to see me?"

"What do you think?"

"Oh, no!" Ron exclaimed. "Do we have to go through all that again? I just recovered from hearing their goodbye up at the Angle."

Aunt Mabel and Kay's mother were walking excitedly about the station wagon.

"It's wonderful," Christine cried. "Think of all the time it will save us, Mabel—all the extra homes and villages we will be able to visit."

"It's an answer to prayer."

Newton Bostwick, who had gotten out of the station wagon, approached them. "My maternal uncle, Harold Forester, purchased the station wagon as a gift for you," he informed them.

For an instant they looked at him quizzically.

"I'm Newton Jonathan Edward Bostwick III," he said. "Apparently the Orlis brothers are too uncouth to introduce me to you."

"I'm sorry," Danny apologized.

"We all forgive you," Ron broke in. "You aren't entirely responsible this evening."

Newton wrinkled his nose. "Your humor is a trifle childish, Ronald."

Ron flushed and turned away.

Danny concluded the introductions then, and

they all got into the station wagon and drove out to the little village where the two missionary women had their home.

Newton snorted when he saw the primitive little hut, built exactly like the Indian huts around it, except that it was larger.

"Do you mean we are going to have to live in that-that hovel?"

"It might be a hovel to you," Aunt Mabel sang out cheerily, "but it's home to us."

He got out and examined it carefully. "I didn't mean to be disrespectful, but after all, it is so."

"Quit your griping, Red," Ron called to him, "and give us a hand with this luggage."

At the dinner table that evening Kay's mother got out the Bible. "You know," she said, "we always come to our Lord when we're in trouble. I think we should come to Him when things have gone well for us, don't you? I think we should thank Him for giving you a safe journey."

"So do I," Danny said fervently.

"I suppose I should resign myself to this childish display of emotionalism," Newton said, sliding his chair back over the rough board floor. "I rather imagine it will be spooned out to me in increasingly nauseating doses."

Kay and her mother and Aunt Mabel stared at him.

"Don't mind him," Ron told them quickly. "He doesn't know the meaning of those words, either."

"Ron," Danny cautioned sternly, "I've asked you several times not to pick on Newton. Now I'm going to insist on it."

The two brothers were staring hard at one another. Finally, Ron's gaze dropped. For a full minute all was still in the little kitchen, then Ron turned to Newton.

"I'm sorry, fella," he said earnestly. "I know it isn't any excuse, but I say stuff because I think it's funny, and I don't mean it at all. I'll try not to pick on you anymore. I sure want to be friends with you."

Newton looked at his outstretched hand, then took it warmly.

Before Christine had an opportunity to find the place in the Bible where she wished to read, there was a loud knock at the door. Mabel went to answer it.

A short, rotund little man, whose face and arms were burned black by the tropical sun, strode into the house. His small, beady eyes shifted nervously as his gaze darted about the room.

"Where is it?" he demanded in a hoarse whisper.

Both Danny and Ron jumped to their feet.

CHAPTER 6

SWITCH ACCOMPLISHED

"What do you mean?" Ron demanded. The strength had suddenly gone out of his knees. The stranger took a step forward.

"Come now," he said crisply, "you can't pull that with me. Where are they? Where are those things you were to bring from Minnesota for Howard Briton?"

"Oh, that," Ron sighed, relief flooding over him.

The man moved closer to him until he was peering at him narrowly, a scant yard away. The pupils of the stranger's eyes protruded grotesquely behind the thick lenses in his horn-rimmed glasses. Almost involuntarily the boy inched backward.

"What else do you have, young man?" he snarled. "What are you keeping from me?"

Danny moved in.

"Just who are you?" he asked sternly, stepping between Ron and the stranger. "And what do you want?"

The little man drew himself up until he stood almost as tall as Ron. "I'm Howard Briton, of course. I thought everyone knew me. And I've come for my lawful possessions."

"Identify them and we'll be glad to turn them over to you."

"Identify them?" he snorted. "How do you identify a spade, or a pick, or a length of rope? We aren't dealing in jewels, young man, or automobiles with serial numbers."

"I'm sorry, Mr. Briton," Danny said, grinning. "I guess the stuff is yours all right."

"I'm glad you have come to your senses. I shall be back for the boxes the first thing in the morning." And then he was gone, stomping resolutely outside without even closing the door.

There was a moment of deep silence.

"That man," Newton said firmly, "is an unmitigated boor."

Laughter rippled across the little group.

"And besides," Ron added, with a quick look at their red-headed companion, "he wasn't a bit nice, especially to me."

"I thought sure you were going to spill the beans about that old book, Ron," Danny said, after a time.

"Aren't you going to give it to him?"

"Not until I'm certain he's the one who's supposed to have it," the older boy replied.

"What are you talking about, Danny?" Kay wanted to know.

Quickly the boys told Kay and the two missionaries what had taken place on the way down to Zongolica, and how they had discovered the copper box and the ancient book.

"That must have been what Mr. Forester was sending down with you," Aunt Mabel said. "Nobody would go to any extra work sending shovels, picks, and ropes down here, even if they are going to make some archaeological exploration. One can buy that sort of thing almost anywhere."

"The book itself is intriguing," Newton broke in, "but as baffling in its way as is the man with the bushy eyebrows. Perhaps more so. It appears to be composed in Latin, but there are some monster words in it which are beyond my comprehension."

"Here it is," Danny said, laying the manuscript on the table before his aunt.

She looked at it carefully. "This is strange," she said.

Newton moved his chair closer to hers and the two of them bent over the scarcely legible writing.

"I have a hunch," Mabel said at last. "There seems to be some sort of pattern here, a-a rhythm, or whatever you wish to call it, that makes me think this might be a translation from another language."

Newton wrinkled his forehead. "Upon what do you base that deduction?"

"Anyone who could write Latin back in the days

when this was written would have known how to write it well. The only conclusion I can draw from this is that he was trying to translate something he had heard or read in another language into Latin. If he were working phonetically, as we do in translating the Bible into some of these Indian dialects, he could get himself involved in some terrific words and combinations of words."

The red-haired lad shook his head admiringly.

"Sister, you've got it!"

She looked at him, amazed. "What did you say?"

He colored fiercely.

"I mean you have an unusual facility with languages and command an uncanny grasp of their internal construction."

Ron snickered. "I've got to hand it to you, Red—I mean Newton—you sure double-talked yourself out of that one."

"I'd like to work on this, Danny," Aunt Mabel said, fingering the book. "It would be fascinating to try to translate it into English."

"Do you think you could?" It was Newton who spoke, eagerly.

"I'm not sure. We're in Mayan territory down here," she continued. "This is only a guess, but since it was sent down into this country I wonder if it doesn't deal with that old Mayan culture, or some other culture of centuries ago."

"What are you going to do?" Newton inquired. "Translate it into Maya, and then English?"

She shook her head. "I'll have trouble enough dealing with English."

For a moment he was crestfallen.

Danny picked up the old book carefully, fingering the yellowed, brittle leaves. "You know, the more I think about it, Aunt Mabel, the more convinced I am that if you can translate this book, we'll know why Bushy Eyebrows is so anxious to get his hands on it."

"Say," Ron broke in, "I just thought of something. If the guy comes back again and sees the box gone, he'll know we found it. He might come into the house after us!"

Kay's face blanched and her mother bit her lower lip.

"I know," Aunt Mabel suggested. "We can gather up some of the worksheets we used when we were translating the Bible into that Indian dialect up at El Diablo. If he isn't a real language student, that might fool him long enough to let you boys get back to the States."

Hurriedly they stuffed the box full of the old worksheets and put the lid into place.

"I'd like to see the fellow's face if he gets hold of this," Christine chuckled. "Of course, he'll know at once that they aren't old, but he'll sweat trying to translate it. I can tell you that much."

Danny turned to Newton. "The Indians at El Diablo didn't even have a written language until

Kay's mother and dad and Aunt Mabel went there, learned to speak their language, and developed a written language."

Newton looked at them with new admiration.

"Kay's dad was killed there. An uprising."

Christine got to her feet. "We're all tired," she said. "I think we should turn in."

"But Mother," Kay reminded her, "we haven't had our devotions yet."

Earlier in the evening Newton had protested sarcastically at the very mention of Bible reading. This time, however, he listened intently, and when the time came for prayer, he bowed his head reverently.

The three boys shared a small room off the kitchen. When they were in bed, the red-headed lad raised up on one elbow.

"You know," he said wistfully, "the Bible must have its fascination if women as intelligent and gifted as Kay's mother and your Aunt Mabel will give their lives to translating it into some obscure Indian dialect."

"It has more than a fascination for them, Newton," Ron answered. "It's the Word of God. It not only tells us what man is like, a lost sinner headed for eternal damnation, but it pleads with us to confess our sins and put our trust in the Lord Jesus so we can be saved."

Newton sighed. "Sometimes you fellows make me wish I had a belief like yours."

"It's easy to have," Ron told him. "The Bible explains it, step by step."

He would have continued the conversation, but Newton rolled over and said no more.

The following morning, they got up and had breakfast, but there was no sign of Howard Briton.

"I thought he'd be here blasting us out of bed before daylight," Ron said.

There was a knock on the door presently, but instead of the rotund little archaeologist, a thin, swarthy Indian lad stood there. He was about the age of Newton and Ron, but a little shorter, and his thin arms looked like parchment-covered sticks.

"My father, he say, Miguel come and help," the Indian lad said in broken English. "He, Juan Hidalgo. Me, Miguel Hidalgo."

"Thank you, Miguel," Aunt Mabel smiled, "but I think we have everything in place now. Tell your father we want to come over as soon as we are settled and thank him for the beautiful little home he built for us."

"He make Miguel help," he said without smiling.

"Then we have you to thank too," Christine put in. "Mr. Morgan tells me you were one of the best students at the school in Zongolica."

Danny and the others wanted to look around a little, but because of Howard Briton they decided to wait.

"We've given him plenty of chance to come this morning," Ron protested. "Make him come back tomorrow."

"That isn't it," his brother said. "I just don't like to leave the women here until we know he isn't going to come around. The more I think about him the less I trust him."

Aunt Mabel thought she would have an opportunity to look at the old book that afternoon, but the day was gone before they knew it, and it was night again.

"I hope that bird comes after his stuff tomorrow," Ron said disgustedly. "I'd like to get a look at this country before we have to go back."

"Me too," Danny answered. "Now choke it off so I can get to sleep."

They must have been in bed and asleep for two or three hours when there was a shout and a loud knock at the door.

"Open!" the voice cried in limping English. "Hurry!"

Kay's mother had slipped into a faded robe and was pulling back the bolt on the heavy, hardwood door when Danny and Ron came running into the kitchen.

"Somebody was outside your car," an old Indian blurted so excitedly that his own dialect spilled over into his English to make an almost unintelligible blur of sound.

Ron felt the color drain from his cheeks. Sweat, cold as ice, beaded his forehead.

Danny grabbed the light from the table and led the group out into the warm night air.

The others went to the doors of the station wagon, but Ron lay on his back and pushed beneath it.

"Is it there?" Danny called, when he saw what Ron was doing.

Ron got to his feet slowly.

"It's gone," he said.

There was a long silence.

"That means he's discovered us," Newton said. The boys hadn't even heard him come up until he spoke. "Bushy Eyebrows found us!"

"No," Ron answered. He looked around to see that Juan Hidalgo, the one who had come to waken them, was talking excitedly with the two missionaries toward the front of the station wagon. "It wasn't the man with the bushy eyebrows. You remember, he knew exactly where to look. Whoever this was almost tore the station wagon apart. Look at those seats, and the door panels!"

"That's right," Danny said, more to himself than to the others. "I wonder what he's going to do when he finds out he doesn't actually have the old book."

Ron swallowed hard.

"I'd never thought of that!"

CHAPTER 7

JUST LOOKING AROUND

Ron and the others went to bed then, but nobody slept much, and shortly after dawn they were all up again.

"I was just wondering, Daniel," Newton began nervously, pausing with a shoe in his hand. "Do you suppose the ravenous individual who pilfered that copper box will perceive our deception?"

Danny shook his head. "He'll discover it, all right, but I don't know when."

"I hope we have completed our sojourn here and will soon transport ourselves to a more tranquil location."

In spite of himself Ron grinned. "You know, Red—I mean Newton," he began, "you should be twins."

"And why, might I inquire?"

"Then one of you could speak and the other could

interpret for a dumb ox like me. Honestly, half the time I don't even know what you're talking about."

"I have been informed by capable authorities that I express myself quite adequately."

"Danny," Kay called from the kitchen. "Breakfast is ready."

Ron turned to the red-haired boy. "Did you hear that, Newton?" he asked, casting a quick glance toward Danny. "You and I are about starved, but does Kay care whether we get anything to eat? Oh, no!" He screwed his face into a prissy little smile and spoke in a high falsetto. "It's, 'Danny, dear, what do you want for breakfast? Should I burn your toast on both sides, or just one, darling? How much lard do I use to fry bacon?'"

"I'm going to lose my temper one of these days, Ron!" Danny warned, trying hard to keep a smile from his lips. "And if I do, I'll massacre you. They'll call it justifiable homicide."

Ron's eyes were dancing.

"Danny, dear, breakfast is ready," he mimicked.

His brother snatched up a shoe and heaved it at him. Ron ducked and scooted out the door.

Before they had an opportunity to sit down to the table there was a loud, aggressive knock at the door, and Howard Briton came swaggering into the kitchen.

"I've come for my boxes."

"Sure thing," Danny told him. "We'll help you load them, won't we, fellows?"

The boxes were heavy, and it was all that the three boys could do to lift them. Nevertheless, Briton stood back, watching as they struggled to hoist the crates into the back of his jeep. When they were finally loaded, he turned to the boys.

"That was fine. Thank you!" He hesitated uncertainly, as though there was more he wished to say to them.

"Tell me, Mr. Briton," Newton began, "just what sort of culture do you expect to find here, Toltec, Mayan, or Aztec?"

A blank look came over Briton's face. "Huh?" he asked.

"What sort of culture do you think you will find when you have finished your archaeological exploration in this area?"

The certainty had gone out of Briton's manner. "A kid like you wouldn't understand them things."

Newton swelled up like a Pouter pigeon. "I'll have you know, Mr. Briton, that I speak and read four languages in addition to English. I have been fascinated with the study of Aztec hieroglyphics, and intrigued with the archaeology of southern Mexico, Honduras, and Guatemala. All leading scholars are certain that the Mayans inhabited this section of North America at one time but are at great variance about the origin of earlier peoples."

"I haven't got time to stand here and argue with you," Briton said lamely. Then he turned to Ron and Danny. "This Mr. Forester in Minnesota," he began. "Did he—"

"He's my uncle," Newton broke in.

"I wasn't talking to you!" He turned back to the Orlis boys. "Did he give you another package for me? Did he say anything about a little packet, about so large?" He indicated the size with his hands.

Danny shook his head. "Nope," he answered. "He just gave us these things for you. It's all on the list."

Briton's forehead wrinkled, and the corners of his mouth twitched.

"I can't understand it," he muttered.

Ron started to speak, but Danny stopped him with a glare. Briton got into his truck and drove away.

Newton stared after him, his hands on his hips. "Were you fellows aware of the fact that our visitor is an impostor? Why, he doesn't know any more about archaeology than a horse knows about calculus."

"I haven't liked him from the very beginning," Danny answered. "Somehow he didn't seem to ring true."

"At least we know this much," Ron said. "Briton isn't the one who stole that copper box with the fake papers."

"Either that or he didn't want us to suspect him," his brother replied.

When the boys got back into the house, Kay and Christine were getting their things together.

"Going somewhere?"

"Just in to Zongolica," Kay answered. "Would you like to go along?"

"Would he?" Ron snorted. "He's just crazy to go to town! All we're going to do is go out into the jungle to do a little exploring. But what's that compared to an exciting trip to Zongolica?"

Danny laughed. "Keep that up, fella, and I'll sic a jaguar or a bushmaster onto you."

"I don't know which would be worse," Ron grunted, "that, or being wrapped around some woman's little finger."

"Just you wait, Ron," Kay chided, smiling. "Your time is coming."

"Come on, Newton," Ron said, "they're both picking on us now. Let's get out of here."

They started down the narrow path toward the little hut where Miguel Hidalgo lived with his parents. He saw them coming and strode out to meet them.

"We thought we'd come over so we could get an early start," Ron said.

Miguel grunted. "Where you want to go?"

Newton stepped forward possessively. "We want you to take us into an area where we can obtain a true perspective of the country and the people," he announced. "We want to learn the customs and culture of your tribe, as well as to obtain an accurate appraisal of the general area."

Miguel's large brown eyes opened wide. There were questions in both of them.

"You struck out on that deal, Red, old boy—I

mean Newton," Ron said. "He lost you way back by home plate."

Miguel faced Ron. "Where you want to go?" he asked again.

"Just take us anywhere. Like my friend here said, we just want to look around."

Miguel started off into the jungle, slowly, but without looking back. Ron and Newton followed closely behind.

As they walked down the narrow, twisting path, it seemed as though they were in a different world than up at the Angle. The trees were there, and the vast silence, which seemed to press down about them like a great, impenetrable cloak, but there the resemblance ended. Instead of evergreens, the huge fronds of the palms waved against the pale blue sky. Vines linked trees together with tough, sinuous arms, and hung down in great profusion. And a giant variety of ferns pushed upward on either side of the path, until it seemed almost to smother them.

"By the way, Miguel," Newton asked when they had walked for half an hour or so, "are there many venomous reptiles in this locality?"

That blank look came into the Indian lad's eyes again.

"No understand."

"You're going to have to talk English, Newt," Ron laughed. "You've got me in up to my ears just trying to tell Miguel what you're driving at."

Ron started to speak, but Newton cut in. "I was asking about the snakes. Do they bite? Do they kill?"

"*Sí*," Miguel answered solemnly. "Have to watch—much close."

When they finally got back to the little village, they thanked Miguel and started back toward the mission house.

"These people are so carefree and happy," Newton began. "Why do the missionaries come down here and bother them? They have their religion, and their culture is so quaint. Why don't the missionaries go back where they came from and leave them alone?"

Ron stopped and faced him.

"The big reason, Newton," Ron began seriously, "is that they are lost. They are headed for damnation forever and ever unless someone brings them the Gospel of the Lord Jesus Christ and they take Him as their Savior."

The red-haired boy thought a moment. "Do you mean to tell me that these people who have never had an opportunity to hear this Gospel, or whatever you call it, are going to Hell?"

"What I say doesn't make any difference, Newton," Ron answered, trying to remember how he had heard Danny and Kay handle that question, "nor what you or Danny or anyone else says. The important thing is this, What does the Bible say? There are a lot of verses that tell us about that. 'All of us like sheep have gone astray'; one of them says, 'There is none righteous, not even one.' Another calls us all sinners, and still another says that the wages of sin is death. There just isn't any way around it, Newton. Anyone in the world, whether he is the poorest, most ignorant Indian, or the most brilliant scientist, is lost for all eternity unless he confesses his sin and puts his trust in the Lord Jesus."

Newton was silent for a long while.

"I don't think I've been so bad," he said defensively.

Ron looked squarely into his eyes. "What does the Bible say?"

* * *

Kay and her mother took longer in town than they had supposed they would, and it was almost dark when they finally came back to the station wagon where Danny was waiting.

Kay was breathless.

"Danny," she said softly as she got into the car beside him, "did you say that car that almost ran you off the road was a black sedan with a Texas license?"

He nodded.

"I just saw it in town," she whispered. "A big man with heavy black eyebrows got into the car and drove up the street slowly. He was staring at the station wagon!"

Danny's eyes widened. "He's found us!"

* * *

When they got home the door was bolted tightly and the blinds were drawn.

"Aunt Mabel!" Danny called. "Ron! Newton! It's us!"

A moment later the blinds moved slightly.

"It's them, all right," they heard Ron say. And then he slipped the bolt and let them in.

"What's the matter?" Danny asked quickly.

Ron motioned over his shoulder. "We were working on that old manuscript," he said. "I mean Newton and Aunt Mabel are working on it. We didn't want anyone to see it."

"Good idea," Danny said, pausing to tell him about Bushy Eyebrows.

Kay went on to the little living room. "How are you coming?" she asked.

Newton didn't even look up.

"We're making a little progress," Aunt Mabel said. "We're beginning to unravel the most exciting story!"

Danny and Ron heard her and came quickly into the room. "Have you found out why everyone's so interested in that old book?" Ron asked.

A tantalizing smile came to her lips.

Newton looked up severely. "We have not completed our translation," he informed them all coldly. "We are not free to make a public statement at this time."

CHAPTER 8

WITH THE CONSPIRATOR

"**C**ome on now," Ron demanded, "don't give us that stuff. We're all in on this thing together, you know."

"When we are ready to confide in you, we will do so, Ronald," Newton said. "Inconclusive results are only confusing."

Ron's face clouded darkly.

Aunt Mabel began to laugh. "Shall we tell them, Newton?" she asked.

"I rather imagine we'll be annoyed to no end until we do."

"The truth of the matter, Ron, is that we have made some major discoveries that will help us with the translation, but we haven't actually learned anything yet."

"You mean he doesn't know any more about it than Danny or me?"

"And neither do I," she laughed.

That evening when the time came for their devotions Newton began to squirm uncomfortably. By the time Kay finished with the Bible reading he could stand it no longer.

"I don't know why you all stare at me the way you do!" Newton blurted, forgetting his five-syllable words in his concern. "Just because I don't go along with this religion of yours doesn't mean I've got leprosy or something. I'm just as good as you are!" With that he leaped to his feet and went bolting into the bedroom.

For almost a minute no one in the little room spoke.

"Have you been talking to him about spiritual things, Ron?" Danny asked at last.

"Sure, a few times."

"He's under conviction," Kay said. The others nodded in agreement.

"We must pray for him," Danny said. "He's a little strange, I know, but that's because he feels so inferior and insecure. Think what a person with a mind like that could do for the Lord."

Christine nodded. "But, of course, the really important thing is to be completely yielded to God. God doesn't have to have a person with a brilliant mind to do big things, but He has to have a completely yielded individual before He can accomplish much of anything with him."

The following morning shortly after breakfast Howard Briton drove up once more.

"I decided I want to talk to you boys again," he said, getting out of his jeep. "Where's that young fellow who was bothering me with all those questions about archaeology?"

Newton came to the door.

"I could use a smart young man like you," Mr. Briton announced. "How would you like to put the books aside and get your hand into some real diggings? They're around here, and we're going to find them."

"Well—"

Briton wiped at his mouth with the back of his grimy hand and took a step toward the red-haired boy.

"To tell you the truth, I've been out of archaeology for quite a spell, and a lot of it got away from me. I could use you to sort of bring me up to date. A fellow gets mighty rusty when he gets away from it for as long as I've been."

"I don't know," Newton said hesitantly.

"The other two fellows can come along too. There's work for all three of you, and you'll be paid mighty well."

"Sounds satisfactory to me," Newton answered.

"Then we'll go too," Danny said quickly.

They got into the jeep beside the pudgy little man and rode in silence to the clearing where Mr. Briton had made camp.

"I'm going to want to talk to you after a while,"

he said to Newton, "but right now there is a great deal of work to do."

That had been no understatement. They worked on the run all day, pitching tents and trenching them, piling the supplies into compact piles and covering them with canvas. When evening finally came Briton told them they would have to walk home.

"I have some important work to do," he said, "but I'll be after you the first thing in the morning."

"What I want to know, Newton," Danny began as soon as they were out of earshot, "is why did you decide to take this job anyway?"

He looked sadly at the blisters on his hands.

"It sounded like a good idea at the time," he said.

"We never would have come over here to work if it hadn't been for you," Danny went on. "I feel uneasy all the time I'm around Mr. Briton."

Newton was silent for a long while. When he spoke, his voice was soft and strained.

"Do you mean you came over here and worked just so I wouldn't be here alone?" he asked. He shook his head disbelievingly.

When they finally reached the village Aunt Mabel was still sitting in the living room with the manuscript.

"I can tell that because the blinds are down and the light's on," Ron said, quickening his pace. "Wonder what she found out?"

Again, the door was locked and Kay had to let them in.

"How's it coming?" Danny asked eagerly.

Newton pulled up a chair and sat down beside her. "Did our conclusions of yesterday assist you in your labors today?"

"It's difficult," she admitted, pushing a few straggling hairs from her forehead, "but I'm beginning to get a little of it."

"All right, all right," Ron said excitedly, "don't keep us in suspense like this. What is it?"

"I'm not sure yet," she said, "but it describes the most fascinating old city and it sounds as though it could be around here somewhere close."

"Old city," Ron echoed. "But why would anyone want to find an old city? It's a certainty there's no one living in it now, or it wouldn't be lost."

"The artifacts," Newton informed him, "would be priceless. In addition to getting evidence that would help archaeologists piece together the story of the civilization which produced the city, there should be a fortune in treasure awaiting the first person to discover it."

"Just listen to this," Aunt Mabel said. "I'm going to translate freely: 'And there were silver vases and ornaments and all manner of utensils overlaid with gold, and within the temple there were objects of gold and silver without number, so many that no accurate count could be kept of them.'"

"D-d-did you hear that?" Ron stammered. "And you say that old city's right down here somewhere?"

"What I can't understand," Christine said, "is why it

hasn't been discovered a long while ago, if it is actually in this area? There are people living all through here."

"Most of them live along or near the roads, Chris," Aunt Mabel said. "And you know that few of them venture very far out into the jungle. Why, it could be within ten miles of where we are right now, and we might spend all our lives here and never stumble onto it."

"But wouldn't it be seen from the air?" Kay asked. "There are a few planes down this way."

"There's an answer to that here too," Aunt Mabel said excitedly. "And the jungle is already swallowing the buildings. Enormous roots are overturning the stone figures. Vines and creepers are spreading along the stairways and terraces, as though to hide the beauty that once had been here."

"And that was written approximately four hundred years ago," Newton added, "as nearly as we were able to determine."

There was a long silence. "Just think what finding something like that could mean for the work of the mission," Chris said, daydreaming. "We could have that new school, a new hospital, and bring in a dozen new workers."

They were still talking when there was a loud knock at the door.

"Quick!" Ron ordered. "Hide that old book!"

Mabel and Kay scooped up the book and worksheets and dashed into the kitchen while the boys went to the door.

Miguel came in, panting, "That man come," he announced. "He ask for you. My father, he say come tell you. Big man. Much big. My father, he no like."

"Did he have heavy eyebrows?" Danny pointed to his own for explanation.

Miguel's forehead wrinkled. "Not know."

Then he was gone, as quickly as he came.

"That's him!" Ron exclaimed. "It's got to be!"

"He's come for that old book," Danny said firmly. "I know it."

Ron's face went ashen. "What are we going to do?"

His brother shook his head. "I don't know, but we're going to have to keep our eyes open from now on. Every minute."

When Briton came after them the next morning Danny asked if they could stay in camp during the night.

"I don't know about that," Mr. Briton hesitated. "You don't want to leave these women alone, do you?"

"We were alone before the boys came to Zongolica," Aunt Mabel told him. "You needn't worry about us."

The work at Briton's camp was harder by far than it had been the day before. As soon as they arrived, he put them to cutting wood and piling it. Danny and Ron both had had a great deal of experience with an ax, but not in such hot weather. The sweat rolled off in great streams and their arms and backs began to throb before the morning was half over.

Newton struggled hard to keep up his end of things, but it was no use. He had never handled an ax or a big saw before and after a couple of hours he dropped exhausted to the ground.

"Briton's not going to like that, Newt," Ron told him, grinning. "He'll think you're lying down on the job."

"He couldn't be more correct," Newton answered. "I'm not only lying down, but I'm to the place where I seriously doubt whether I shall ever be able to get my limbs under me again."

"Did you ever see so much stuff?" Ron asked, wiping the sweat from his forehead. "Why do you suppose he's got all those big ropes and chains and crowbars, and that heavy iron-wheeled cart?"

"Artifacts are often exceedingly heavy," Newton informed him importantly. "And if statuary should be found it would undoubtedly be of very great value."

"Well, if the stuff's any heavier than what we've been lugging I hope they don't find any."

Ron had expected Briton to fly into a rage when he came back and saw Newt lying in the grass. But instead, he looked down at him and chuckled dryly.

"So, it got the best of you, eh?" he asked. "I've been wanting to talk to you, anyway. Do you think you can make it over to my tent?"

Newton looked up at him impishly. "Would it be too much trouble, Mr. Briton," he asked, "to bring your tent over here?"

"Come on, Red," Ron broke in, striding over to where his companion was lying. "I'll help you up." As he bent over, he whispered in Newton's ear. "You lucky stiff! I didn't think you'd pull a goldbricking deal like this on me. And to think you're getting away with it!"

Newton got painfully to his feet and brushed at his trousers with his swollen, blistered hands.

"I think I can make it to the tent, thank you, Ronald," he said with great deliberation. "I must endeavor to do so without your assistance. I wouldn't want to take you from your work."

Ron made a face at him.

By the time night came, Danny and Ron were so tired and sore they could scarcely move.

Briton squatted down beside them and pushed another branch in the fire.

"We've taken the work a little easy today," he said, "but now that you're toughened into it, we should get something done tomorrow."

Ron stared at him incredulously.

"What I want to know," Ron asked after a time, "is what on earth are you ever going to do with all that wood?"

Briton looked at him and grinned. "It might get cold some of these days," he said.

When they had finished dinner around the campfire Danny took out his Bible and began to finger through it.

"Why don't you read aloud?" Ron asked him.

Newton, who was sitting across from them, began to squirm uneasily, but he said nothing.

In a moment or two Danny began to read from one of Paul's letters in a loud, clear voice. Briton stirred uneasily.

"I don't know why you have to read that stuff," Newton muttered under his breath when Danny had finished. "There's nothing to it anyway."

"It's the Word of God," Ron told him.

"All that talk of sin and salvation. It's enough to keep a fellow worked up all the time."

Newton's face was ashen.

"Well, I'm going to turn in," Briton told them, getting to his feet. "And I think you fellows had better do the same. We're going to start work awfully early in the morning."

They got into their sleeping bags in a short time and closed their eyes. It seemed as though Danny and Newton fell asleep almost instantly; but Ron lay there, looking up at the heavy canvas tent above them, and peeking out through the mosquito netting front at the stars that seemed to hang suspended a few feet above the tops of the trees.

Newton was under conviction. Ron was sure of that. He had recognized that strained, haunted look in the red-haired lad's eyes, and the longing that flickered there when he thought no one was watching. If only there was something he could do, something he could say. For a long while he prayed, until finally he drifted off to sleep.

He must have been asleep only a few moments when he heard a soft footstep outside his tent. He raised up on one elbow, drowsily, listening.

"You sure took your time about coming, Joe." It was Briton, his loud voice echoing through the still jungle.

"I came as fast as I could, Bart," the other voice answered. "Had to wait till those kids fell asleep. Why did you let them stay here?"

"There wasn't any way to get out of it. Anyway, I didn't know you'd be in today. You don't have to worry about them. I worked them so hard their tongues were dragging. One of them, that smart cookie, didn't last more than a couple of hours. He's done in right now, and in a couple of days I'll have the other two so worn out we won't have to worry about them getting in our hair."

"I don't like having them here, Bart," Joe answered. "We've got too much at stake to run any risks we don't have to."

"You don't need to worry about that. I'm taking care of them. When they're here I can keep my eye on them, and I know what they're doing."

"All right," the stranger agreed hotly, "but I don't want them to see us together."

"There isn't any danger out here in the middle of the night," Briton retorted. "And besides, I got those papers, and I've been working on them, but something's gone wrong!"

"Now don't try to give me that! I don't double-cross easily!"

"I'm telling you the truth. I got that fellow who had promised to translate them for you, but he couldn't do a thing with them. He said he didn't even know what language they were written in!"

"That book's in Latin," Joe countered. "I saw it myself about two years ago."

"This fellow said it wasn't," Briton answered, "and he said they weren't old, either."

Joe's voice had taken on a new, ominous tone. "Listen," he said, "I know that old book was put in that copper box and fastened under the station wagon. I know those kids brought it down here. I almost got it myself the first night after they arrived in Mexico. If you're trying to double-cross me, you'll never double-cross anyone else again!"

Ron crouched there, tensely. He couldn't breathe. He couldn't move! What if they learned what had happened?

CHAPTER 9

A SECRET CAVE?

For a long while Ron crouched there, straining to hear what the two men were saying. His heart was hammering a fierce tattoo in his throat and the sweat had come out on his forehead in great, glistening drops. He cast a quick look in the darkness toward his sleeping companions.

By this time Joe and Briton, or Bart, or whatever his name was, had walked down the path out of hearing.

"Danny," Ron whispered cautiously, "Newt, wake up!" The two boys stirred restlessly.

"Wake up," Ron whispered again, "and whatever you do, be quiet about it."

Newton was mumbling sleepily, but Danny sat up, rubbing at his eyes.

"What's the matter, Ron?"

"Why don't you let a fellow sleep?" Newton muttered, still more asleep than awake. "It is quite annoying to be awakened so rudely in the middle of the night."

"Cut the double-talk, Red," Ron retorted irritably. "This is important. Bushy Eyebrows was just here."

"What?" Danny and Newt exclaimed, almost at the same time.

"That's right, only Briton called him Joe."

"I knew we shouldn't be trusting that guy," Danny said.

"And," Ron continued softly, the words tumbling over one another in their haste to be out, "he called Briton, Bart something or other. I don't think the guy who called himself Briton to us was even supposed to have those supplies. He's an impostor."

"And to think," Newton said, "I punished my poor hands and back unmercifully for him."

"Yeah," Ron broke in, "for about an hour. I never saw such a goldbricker."

"The difficulty with you, Ronald," Newton replied smugly, "is that you are angry that I thought of it first."

Ron started to reply, but his brother punched him sharply in the ribs. "They're coming back," he whispered.

Silently the boys scooted down into their sleeping bags and lay there tensely, listening.

"I'm going to check with that translator the first thing in the morning," Joe was saying as they passed the boys' tent. "If we did get the wrong manuscript, we've got to find the genuine article pronto. There isn't any time to lose."

Briton went back to his tent then, and in a few minutes the boys could hear his heavy, regular breathing. But try as they would, sleep would not come. They were still awake when the first rays of dawn came creeping through the trees.

"Now watch your step, Newt," Ron whispered as the boy was about to leave the tent. "We don't want Briton to get wise."

"Have no fear, Ronald," Newton told him, "I shall be the very epitome of caution."

"That guy bothers me with those big words, Danny," Ron muttered under his breath. "I keep wondering if he's talking about me."

"We'd better quit our jobs this morning, Ron," Danny whispered. "Get word to Newton without letting Briton hear you."

Ron nodded casually.

They were up almost an hour earlier than usual, but Briton already had a fire built and was cooking breakfast.

"What are you fellows trying to do," he demanded, "sleep all day?"

Newton looked at his watch. "It is now fifty-seven minutes and thirty-nine seconds earlier than we arose yesterday morning." He put the watch back in his pocket. "That is exactly one hour three minutes and thirty-nine seconds earlier than you told us to arise."

The man whirled and lashed out at him. "I know when I told you to get up. Here—" He took his billfold from his pocket. "Take your pay and get out of here."

Before they quite realized what was happening they had their money and were walking toward the Indian village where the missionaries lived.

"That guy must be a mind reader," Ron said. "Here we were all set to quit, and before we get the chance, we get canned."

"We've got to hurry," Danny said, quickening his pace. "When they find out we switched those papers for that old book there's no telling what they'll do!"

Although the trip to Briton's camp from the village had seemed short enough in the jeep, it was midmorning when the boys finally reached the mission house.

"I am quite famished," Newton said as they rounded a bend in the road and saw the scattered huts of the little village.

"There's something more important than eating right now," Danny said, almost breaking into a run.

Aunt Mabel had put the old book aside and Christine and Kay were sitting with her in the living room.

"Are you alright?" Danny asked as he burst into the room. "Has anything happened?"

"Happened?" Kay echoed. "What do you mean? Nothing unusual has happened here."

"Then we're in time. We've got to get that old book hidden in a place where it can't possibly be found!"

Hurriedly he and Ron and Newton told them of the events the night before.

"So they'll be coming here looking for that old book," Ron put in, "just as soon as the translator tells them they've been duped."

"Perhaps it would be expedient for all of us to remove ourselves to the mission headquarters in Zongolica," Newton suggested. "Discretion, we are informed, is the better part of valor."

"We could go there for a while," Christine told him. "But we have our work. We can't let that slide."

His eyes narrowed. "Do you mean to inform me that you would-would risk being harmed in order to preach this Gospel, or whatever you call it, to a village of ignorant Indians?"

"They are lost, Newton," Kay told him, "and if we don't tell them of the Lord Jesus and His saving grace, they might never have an opportunity for salvation."

He shook his head, and Ron saw that peculiar, haunted look return to his eyes. He would have said something, but Newton turned quickly away.

"We've got to get that book hidden, Aunt Mabel," Danny told her. "Those fellows are apt to be here any time."

She picked up the old book and disappeared into the kitchen, then she ran quickly to the bedroom. In a moment she was back.

"Is it securely hidden?" Newton asked her.

"We've had experience hiding things before," she told him, smiling. "I'm sure they'll never find it."

The following morning the boys, Kay, and Aunt

Mabel, with Miguel to guide, went out to visit among the Indian families.

"Why you come here and preach to us?" Miguel demanded as soon as they started down the trail. "We have good religion. You leave us alone." He scowled darkly.

"Your father knows the Lord Jesus as his Savior, Miguel," Danny informed him gently.

"I'm afraid you don't comprehend, Miguel," Newton said. "These people have come here to help you. They are your friends."

Ron turned quickly. "Do you know what you just said, Newton?" he asked so softly none of the others could hear.

Newton Bostwick's lips were twitching nervously. "I just couldn't stand to hear him rip into these women who are giving up everything to come out and preach to them. I don't believe I ever saw anyone so unappreciative!"

Ron was looking at him fixedly. "I have," he said without raising his voice. "The Lord Jesus Christ came to this earth as man, lived without sin and died on the cross so that men and women and boys and girls could have eternal life. If we haven't taken that gift of His, if we haven't confessed our sin and put our trust in Him, doesn't that make us even more unappreciative than Miguel? He didn't only give up a nice Home. He gave up the glories of Heaven, and finally gave His life. If we ignore His gift, what does that make us?"

Newton stared at him, blinking rapidly. Then the color rushed to his cheeks. "Leave me alone, will you?" he demanded loudly. "Leave me alone!"

It was two or three miles through the dense, swampy jungle to the first little Indian hut.

"The man here, he work in the States once, long time ago," Miguel told them. "He speak English."

A short, swarthy Mexican Indian came to the door.

"What you want?"

"We'd like to talk to you for a few minutes," Aunt Mabel said pleasantly.

"Why you come here?" he persisted.

"We're from the new mission," she began, "the evangelicals."

Anger flashed in the dark eyes. "Go home," he told them curtly. "We have church. We have religion. You leave us alone."

Ron and Newton backed off a step or two, almost involuntarily, seeing the man's wrath.

For a brief instant, the man glared at them. Then he stepped back and slammed the door until the windows rattled. Miguel nodded approvingly.

"You can't blame them," Kay said gently as they started down the jungle path toward the next home. "We'll just have to pray a little harder for them. Think what a joy it is when you can finally break through that resentment and win a person to the Lord."

Aunt Mabel smiled weakly. "I guess that's the only

thing that keeps us going," she said. "It's certainly discouraging at times."

Toward evening they made their last call and went wearily back to the village. Christine was just setting the table.

"Oh, yes," Newton said when they were all seated at the table and had begun to eat, "I meant to query you concerning your progress with the translation, Aunt Mabel. Were you able to decipher any more of the old book while we were slaving for the enemy?"

"Didn't I tell you about it?" she asked. "I guess I was so excited when you came bursting in yesterday, insisting that we hide the book right away, that I completely forgot about it."

"But what progress did you make?" he persisted.

"I was able to get a little more of it, Newton," she told him, "but I'm afraid I've reached the limit of my Latin. It is apparently more scrambled and confused toward the middle of the book. It gives me a terrible headache just to look at it."

"But what did you find out?" Ron asked her. "That's what we want to know."

"I think I got some more on the location of this old city," she informed them. "But I came across something even more fascinating—in a horrible sort of way."

"Now what do you mean by that?" Ron wanted to know.

"The book tells about a sacred cave where the old priests used to perform human sacrifices."

"Human sacrifices?" Kay demanded, shuddering.

"That was quite common in ancient religions," Newton added. "There seems to be a period in the histories of most people when human beings were sacrificed, usually unmarried girls about your age, Kay."

"How terrible!"

"Whenever there was a drought," Aunt Mabel continued, "or when it rained for an excessively long period of time, or if anything terrible in the way of storms or tidal waves happened, the priests would say that it was because the gods were angry. They would choose half a dozen beautiful young maidens and take them into the cave. According to the account there is a drop of a hundred feet or more somewhere in the cave. They used to throw girls off that, to the rocks below."

Kay gasped again.

"It just goes to show what some of these pagan religions actually are," her mother put in.

"But where is this old city supposed to be?" Ron broke in. "How do we go about finding it?"

"Yes," Newton added. "Are the directions explicit enough for us to follow them?"

"There are some directions," Aunt Mabel answered, "but I don't know how well you'll be able to follow them."

CHAPTER 10

THE ANCIENT CITY FOUND!

They sat there for a space of time, tensely, every eye on Aunt Mabel. A tantalizing smile toyed with the corners of her mouth. She started to speak again, then paused.

"Don't tell me we're going to have to coax you, Aunt Mabel," Ron exclaimed, exasperated. "Come on, out with it. Red—I mean Newt—and I are about to pass out with excitement."

"We are all most interested in learning the contents of the translation," Newton told her, "if you have progressed far enough so that you feel safe in divulging the information."

"You've got us all anxious, Aunt Mabel," Danny said.

"I shouldn't have made so much of it," she said, smiling slightly. "I've already told you most of it. The book does give a rather good picture of the country around the city. It pinpoints it by telling how far it is from the river, and what the mountains and hills nearby are like."

"Do you really think we could find it?" Ron asked.

Newton drew himself up and turned to face the young boy. "I am quite positive, Ronald," he said smugly, "that if Aunt Mabel has correctly translated the portion which describes the location of the old city, I will be able to follow the directions well enough to find it."

Ron flushed a little. "That's just dandy," he said, his voice fringed with ice. "It's good to know that you've made yourself such an authority on the jungle. We've been here almost a week, you know."

"Directions are directions, no matter where you find them."

"These directions don't sound so difficult," Aunt Mabel went on. "The book tells us that the city is just over the first range of mountains which overlook the sea. It is supposed to be near the place where the Piedras River joins the Diego Vedendre River."

"Why, that should be easy to find," Danny broke in.

"Too easy," Ron added.

"And what do you mean by that?" Newton asked him.

"It seems to me that it's too easy to find for it to still be undiscovered," the boy continued. "There's no reason why anyone would miss finding it if they had those directions and ever tried to look for it. And we're surely not the first ones who have translated part of that old book. You can bet on that."

Danny was crestfallen.

"The difficulty is," Newton answered, "that no one took this book seriously, nor the author, for that matter."

"Now you tell us," Ron scoffed. "And how did you get to be an authority on this book so suddenly?"

"By reading the clipping in the back," Newton said, taking on himself a superior smile. "The clipping describes the book and tells that the author described the splendor of the cities in southern Mexico with such detail, and in such glowing terms that they could not possibly be true."

"Then there isn't anything to it," Ron concluded. "I guess we should have known."

"That doesn't necessarily follow," Newton informed him. "The authorities thought the same thing about another Indian scholar who wrote about the Toltecs who formerly lived in the area where Mexico City now is. Nobody thought his account was true either, until an archaeologist decided to make a search some years ago. To everybody's surprise except his own, he found the city just exactly as it had been described."

Ron sighed. "I can hardly wait until tomorrow."

The following morning, they had all intended to make the trip to the place where the rivers joined. An old, almost abandoned road would take them to within seven or eight miles of the place.

"The area between the road and the river has apparently not been mapped," Newton announced, studying the map intently after breakfast. "While that is going to make our journey a bit more hazardous, it is one more piece of evidence that no one has combed the area where the city is supposed to be hidden."

"You know, Newt, being so smart would bother me," Ron said with grudging admiration. "Aren't you afraid you'll blow a blood vessel in your brain or something?"

The little group was just finishing their morning devotions when one of the natives came running up excitedly.

"My wife, she much sick," he blurted, "she die if you no come. Quick!" He indicated, gesturing, that he wanted both Mabel and Chris.

"I'll get my first aid kit," Aunt Mabel said.

Kay's face clouded. "I was counting so much on going over there this morning, Mother," she said. "Do you suppose it would be all right if I go along?"

Christine thought a moment, frowning. "There will only be boys," she said, "and I don't like that. The people may not understand."

"Going with Danny is different, Mother," she said. "It isn't like going out with just any boy." She looked at Ron. "And besides, I feel like a big sister to the others. I could help Danny take care of them."

Ron snorted contemptuously.

"I think it would be all right, Kay," her mother answered.

It was not far to the sick Indian woman's house, so Aunt Mabel and Christine walked through the jungle with the distraught husband.

"This is style," Ron exclaimed, climbing into the rear seat of the station wagon with Miguel and Newton, while Danny and Kay got in front.

Miguel shook his head.

"The spirits not like this," he muttered softly. "It make them angry. Much angry."

Newton turned toward him. "Do you mean to tell me that you believe in evil spirits in this enlightened age, Miguel?" he asked.

"Spirits not like."

"I thought you had a religion," Ron said to the Indian lad. "You told me you go to church. Why are you afraid of evil spirits? Doesn't your religion have the power to protect you from them?"

Hesitation flickered in Miguel Hidalgo's dark eyes.

"You should put your trust in the Lord Jesus Christ, Miguel," Ron said seriously.

They had covered three or four miles. The road kept getting steadily worse, and Danny put the station wagon into second gear. The trees, that had once been cleared out for quite a distance on either side, had in the past several years crowded in against the narrow, rutted roadway.

"Have you noticed how much happier your father is, Miguel," Ron asked presently, "since he took Christ as his Savior? Haven't you seen how his face shines, and how much better he treats your mother?"

The Indian boy scowled.

"My father will bring the curse upon us all," he retorted grimly. "Already the corn begins to burn, and the javelina are scarce."

Once or twice, Ron tried to talk to him again, but he only grunted in reply.

At last, they reached the place where the road narrowed almost to a path. Danny stopped.

Newton leaned forward, looking toward the jungle with some apprehension. "I assume we will have to walk the balance of the distance to our destination."

"If you get there, you're going to walk," Ron laughed. "We surely will not carry you."

"You watch for snakes now," Miguel warned as they crawled out of the station wagon.

"Snakes?" Ron echoed. "That's a nice, cheerful thought."

Newton stood there for an instant, looking about, then started toward the jungle.

"Just a minute," Danny called, locking the car door. "We aren't ready to go in there yet. Let's have prayer before we go." Quietly they bowed their heads as Danny led in prayer. Then he took his compass from his pocket and checked the directions carefully.

"And what is the purpose behind this, may I ask?" Newton queried.

"It would be nice to get back here," Danny said.

"And we will, if we get oriented so we can make a map as we go into the jungle. That's the cardinal law of any wilderness country."

When he had his bearings and had marked the road on one corner of a piece of stiff paper, they went into the jungle. Danny wrote down the time and the direction they were going.

What the natives had said about the triangular piece of ground between the two rivers was true. The forest around the mission station had been thick enough, but this was like a tangled, almost impenetrable screen of vines, scrubby brush, and trees.

They hadn't realized they had left the station wagon on high ground until they plunged downward sharply, a hundred yards or so back of the road. Farther on they found swampland. They could smell it before they got to it, the faint musty odor of stale water and decaying vegetable matter. Ron plunged into it first, without warning. The murky water came to his knees.

"Hey!" he cried. "I found that swamp!"

"You watch for snakes," Miguel warned. "This—" He stopped suddenly. "Stand still!"

Ron froze, his eyes wide with terror.

Quickly the Indian boy snatched up a heavy branch and crept forward.

"EEEyi!" he shouted. His arm darted out, and in an instant a great copperhead was writhing on the ground, almost at Ron's feet. Miguel clubbed him again, and the snake moved no more.

Ron stepped back uncertainly and wiped at his forehead with a trembling hand.

"Thanks, Miguel," he managed to say. "I didn't even see that fellow until you shouted to me."

"Better you should let Miguel go first," the Indian boy announced.

With that they traded places.

All morning and afternoon they tramped wearily through the swamp, dragging their feet up out of the stagnant water, and stumbling over deadfalls, and hopeless tangles of vines and brush. Their hands and faces were scratched, and their bones protested in agony. Finally, two hours or so before dark, they turned back.

The next day it was the same, and the next. Kay, who had started out so determinedly, missed the second and third days, unable to force herself to go along.

"I just can't do it, Danny," she told him. "I want to go, but I know I'd give out before we went two miles."

"It's rough, all right. I'm beginning to doubt whether either Miguel or the book know anything."

She was silent.

"We'll try it one more day," Danny said, "and then I'm in favor of forgetting the whole thing. All we've got for proof that there is a city out there is an old book that was written four hundred or five hundred years ago."

While they had been talking, Newton got out a large map of the area, and he and Ron bent over it.

"There is our difficulty, Daniel," Newton exclaimed suddenly, pointing. "We stopped the station wagon at approximately this point. Actually, we should proceed on foot to the very summit of the ridge. Let's see, that would be about two miles farther. And then we should go west to enter the swamp. The difficulty is that the river takes a sharp turn down there where we've been making our search. It must be all of twenty miles over to the river at that point, while it's only six or eight miles up here."

Danny scratched his head thoughtfully.

"I believe you're right at that."

Everyday Aunt Mabel and Kay's mother thought they would be able to make the trip into the jungle, but first one thing prevented them, and then another.

"But I'm going to try it again, anyway," Kay said. "I think I can make it this time."

"You just think we're going to find it this trip," Ron chided, "and you want to be in on the excitement."

"How did you ever guess?"

They still had to leave the car in the same spot and walk up the ridge. The road dwindled to a trail, and then a path. A deer bounded across the path not far ahead of them, as they walked silently along, while monkeys chattered wildly in the treetops on either side.

A bit farther on, a huge tapir, looking much like one of Minnesota's black bears, except for its long, curved snout and sleek coat, poked its head timidly out of the jungle. Ron and Newton both turned suddenly.

Kay laughed.

Finally, they reached the top of the ridge and Miguel guided them off the trail toward the west.

The swamp was still almost impenetrable.

"I almost wish I'd stayed at home," Kay said, after stumbling along beside Danny for two or three hours.

"The river is close now," Miguel assured her. "I can hear the water."

Newton wrinkled his nose. "You must be mistaken."

"I hear water."

The Indian boy walked ahead of them, motioning for them to follow. They had scarcely walked a dozen yards when they broke through the tangle of green to see the murky, sluggish river. Miguel said nothing, but he turned with some deliberation and faced Newton.

"Now in which direction do we go?" Ron asked.

"Upstream, of course," Newton broke in. "The directions were explicit."

As they traveled upstream the ground began to rise gently. Almost before they knew it, they were out of the swamp and on solid ground.

"That's a relief," Ron sighed deeply.

Kay turned to speak to him. As she did so she stopped. Her mouth dropped open and, for a moment, she stared wordlessly.

"What's the matter?" Danny demanded.

"Look!" She was pointing a shaking finger.

There, before their eyes, lay the ruins of a dozen or more ancient stone buildings!

"We've found it!" Ron Orlis cried.

CHAPTER 11

AN UNEXPECTED CALLER

A moment of tense, expectant hush settled over the little group. Even the everpresent monkeys, and the parrots, seemed to stop their chattering. Miguel's face had gone a pasty yellow. He muttered unintelligibly under his breath. Ron started to speak, but the words clung to the roof of his mouth. He gulped and moistened his lips.

"Danny," Kay trembled, taking hold of his arm without realizing it, "I just can't believe that it's true! I—" Her voice failed her.

"It's true, all right," he said. "But somehow I don't believe I really ever expected to find it."

"Th-th-that cave," Ron managed. "Now if we can just find it!"

Danny and Kay both nodded, wordlessly.

The buildings had indeed been large. Even by today's standards they could not have been called small. Parts of some of the walls were still standing, like ghastly sentinels of the ravages of time. A whole room of one building stood intact, even to the roof. And across the way, on a steep hill there were great steps which went up to what could have been the beginning of a huge pyramid, or the ruins of an ancient temple. Gigantic stone columns were intricately carved with figures and designs. Three minutes passed, and then five. Newton, who had been silent ever since Kay first saw the city, took a step or two forward and raised his voice dramatically.

"We have at this moment taken history by the hand," he intoned like some ancient orator on the steps of the Parthenon in Athens. "Who knows? Perhaps one day my name will be inscribed in the everlasting granite of one of these ancient buildings for all posterity to see."

Ron snickered. "They'll never do it, Red," he replied. "Newton Jonathan Edward Bostwick III. These buildings are already wrecks. Think what carving a name like that would do to what's left."

Kay took a step or two forward, hesitantly. "Do you suppose we dare go over there?" she asked, her voice still trembling.

Danny moved up beside her.

"What I can't figure out," he said softly, as they continued to walk toward the old buildings, "is how they ever got those columns up there? They must be ten or eleven feet high, and probably weigh that many tons."

By this time, they had drawn close enough to see the carvings clearly.

"What are they?" Kay asked.

"They look like snakes to me," Ron answered.

Newton nodded wisely. "Many of the ancient religions used the symbol of the snake. Often it represented one of their gods."

"I wonder if there's anything significant in that," Ron said thoughtfully. "You know Satan appeared to Eve in the form of a serpent in the garden of Eden. And most pagan religions seem to be Satan worship, or something very close to it."

"That's something I had never thought of, Ron," Danny said. "It does seem strange to find people who worship snakes or a carving of a snake."

Newton had left the others and was moving among the gigantic columns. "It is very simple to see why this city has not been observed from the air," he announced with the voice of authority. "The trees have grown up among them, and the ferns and grass have grown in the mud that washed down off the hills to help make an almost perfect camouflage." He walked back to where Danny and the others were standing. "Unless, of course, a plane should happen to fly directly over it at low altitude."

The little group had been so excited at the discovery of the ancient city that they had not remembered Miguel until that very moment.

"Where is he?" Ron asked, looking quickly about. "What happened to him?"

Newton's eyes widened. "Who?" he demanded.

"Miguel! We'll never be able to make it back to the place where we left the station wagon!"

"I don't think he's gone far," Danny said. With that he cupped his hands to his mouth.

"Miguel!" he called. The words echoed and re-echoed through the jungle. "Miguel!"

There was no answer.

"W-w-what are we going to do?" Newton asked, his gaze turning cautiously into the jungle around them.

"Miguel!" Danny shouted once more. "Where are you?" There was no answer, but in a moment or two the Indian boy came slowly, reluctantly, out of the tangle of vines and brush.

"You shouldn't have left us like that, Miguel," Danny said sternly. "We didn't know what had happened to you."

"The spirits no like that we come," he protested. "They much angry."

"We aren't going to worry about the spirits. They aren't going to harm us."

Miguel was unconvinced.

"It getting dark now," he stammered, his dark brown cheeks were pale. "We go. It much better not to be here in the dark."

"I'm not worried about the spirits," Ron said, "but I go along with Miguel on that night business. I sure don't want to be anywhere around this place after the sun goes down."

"The dangers of remaining here after nightfall are negligible," Newton said. "I should have no qualms about it at all if necessity required it."

"It's different with me," Ron told him. "They aren't going to carve my name on one of these rocks."

Danny looked up at the sky. The sun was already dangerously low in the west, and darkness that far south came like the dropping of a curtain to blot out the light.

"I'm not afraid to be here," he said, "but I do think it would be better for us to get out of here before dark. We might have a rough time finding our way back if we don't."

That was enough for Miguel. He turned, and almost ran back in the direction from which they came.

"Do you suppose we can remember how to get back here Danny?" Ron asked, falling into step beside his brother.

"Of course," Danny replied. "It won't be any trouble at all. I've already got the landmarks spotted. We should be able to walk right to it tomorrow."

Miguel was traveling just short of a run. He had his head down and was plowing determinedly through the swamp as though his very life depended upon every passing moment.

"I didn't see any of that gold and silver that was supposed to be lying around everywhere, Danny," Ron said as they left the swamp and began to make their way up the steep slope to the path that had once been the end of a road. "Or do you suppose, maybe, this was a holiday, and they had the stuff locked in the bank?"

"You didn't expect to find any gold and silver out in the open, did you?" his brother asked. "We won't find anything like that until we get to digging around the ruins."

"I can hardly wait to get into that old room that's still standing," Kay put in.

"Isn't that just like a woman?" Ron asked disdainfully.

"What do you know about girls?" Danny queried.

"Listen," the younger boy told him, "I got one for a twin. And I know all there is to know about them. Turn Roxie loose in some old attic and she's like a tomcat at a mouse convention."

"I'd still like to get into that room," Kay laughed.

"We'll take you there and leave you," Ron continued, "and I'll bet after we've finished digging out the whole city you'll still be there, poking around."

"Your alleged humor is quite droll for an unsophisticated mind, Ronald," Newton said, "but this is scarcely the place for it. What are we going to do if our former employer and his friend, Joe, begin to snoop around? How are we going to prevent them from discovering our secret?"

They stopped beside the station wagon. "The best thing we all can do," Danny cautioned, "is to keep absolutely mum about this. Don't say anything to anybody." He addressed the Indian boy. "You won't tell anyone, will you, Miguel?"

Their dark-skinned guide shook his head. "Not Miguel. He no tell."

"Fine. I know we can depend upon you."

The others started to get into the station wagon. "We not go there again, do we?" Miguel asked, hanging back. "We not go back."

"The first thing in the morning," Danny told him. "We've got to go over those buildings carefully."

The Indian boy put his hand on his stomach and grimaced. "I sick. I much sick."

"You'll feel better when we get home."

When they had ridden two or three miles, Miguel turned to Ron. "Your Jesus. He protect Miguel? Me give gift to Him, and He protect?"

Ron shook his head. "We can't come to Jesus that way, Miguel," he said, struggling to find words, "and buy His care and protection. We must come to Him because we know that we are sinners and need a Savior, that we are lost and will spend eternity in Hell unless we confess our sins and put our trust in Him. We can't buy His friendship and care like your people might try to buy the favor of one of their gods."

Miguel turned the matter over slowly in his mind.

"My father, he say Jesus watch close after him. All time he pray. Jesus take care of him."

"That's after you have taken Him as your Savior, Miguel," Ron tried to explain. "Salvation is a gift. The Bible tells us that we can't earn it. We must put our trust in the Lord Jesus for it, confessing our sin and depending upon Him to save us."

The Indian boy seemed not to understand, but surprisingly, Newton Bostwick turned to him.

"I don't think I have ever heard salvation explained like that before, Ron," he said. There was a tone never heard in Newt's voice before. All the affectation and pose were gone, and a new note of sincerity had taken their place. "Is it really as simple as that to become a Christian?"

"That's right, Newt," Ron replied. "The trouble is we try to make it too complicated. The Bible explains salvation in terms so simple that even a child too young to go to school can understand. But that doesn't mean it isn't important. It's the most important thing in the world."

Newton sat back and turned his face toward the window. "You've given me something to think about." His voice broke a little, and Ron noticed that Newt was swallowing hard.

While Ron was searching for words Danny pulled up before the mission house. "Now," he said, "to tell Aunt Mabel and Kay's mother about our find."

While Danny went around to open the door for Kay, Ron jumped out and motioned to Newt. "Come on, let's beat them to it."

The two boys ran up to the house and flung open the kitchen door. "Guess what we found!" Ron sang out. "Guess—" He stopped abruptly, staring at the tall, handsome stranger who was seated at the table across from Aunt Mabel and Kay's mother.

"Hello there," the man said genially, getting to his feet and holding out his hand. "I suppose you thought I'd never get here."

Ron and Newton turned to look at Danny who had just come into the kitchen with Kay. Questions stood full in their eyes.

"What-what do you mean?" Danny stammered.

"You remember," the man went on, "you brought some things down from Minnesota for me. Or at least I hope you did. I'm Howard Briton!"

Sudden silence settled over the little kitchen, choking off conversation the way a big storm cloud smothers the wind for a tortured heartbeat before it strikes. Newton Bostwick's freckles stood out like blotches of brown ink against the pasty white of his face. Ron was biting his lower lip and clenching his fists nervously.

"How-Howard Briton?" he managed to say at last.

"That's right," the stranger answered. "I'm the archaeologist from the University of Southwest Texas. A friend of mine who knew the chap who furnished the station wagon you fellows drove down here asked him to get some things for me in the States. I should have been here a week or so ago," he explained, "but I was unavoidably detained."

"You-you mean you're Howard Briton?" Ron repeated.

"What's so strange about that?"

"N-n-nothing," Ron blurted. "Only another guy came here the night after we did. We gave the stuff to him."

Anger flickered in the newcomer's eyes. "Didn't you have instructions to keep it for me?" he demanded. "Didn't this Mr. Forester tell you the supplies were for Howard Briton?"

"Of course he did," Danny explained. "But this other fellow knew all about the shipment and everything. He told us that he was Briton, so we gave the things to him."

Briton pursed his lips. "I should have known." He leaned forward. "It isn't the supplies that we really cared about, anyway. But what about the book. Did they get it?"

"Harold Forester didn't say anything about a book," Danny countered. "In fact, he gave us a list and said that was all we had."

"That's all he knew about. We didn't even dare to take him into our confidence. But actually, the book is all that we care about. The other things were just a blind. Did this-this impostor get the book? That's what I want to know."

"Why is it so important?" Danny asked him without answering his question. "What's it like?"

"I've never seen it personally," Briton answered. "But they tell me that it is a rather poor attempt to translate Mayan into Latin. The author attempted to do it phonetically and ran into all sorts of difficulties. Words are run together, and Latin punctuation and sentence structure are abused horribly. But we have reason to believe that it contains the key to all archaeological exploration in this section of Central America."

"How did you come to send it with us?" Ron asked.

"A fellow in Minnesota who collects old books had it. We made arrangements to borrow it, but before we got it, news leaked out and certain other interests learned of its importance. So we hit on the idea of putting it in a copper box and wiring it under the frame of the station wagon. The customs' authorities knew it was coming through. They were supposed to give you a police escort, or at least have officers follow closely behind you, but there was a foul up of some sort." He stopped and got to his feet. "There. Does that convince you that the book is intended for me? Where is it? What have you done with it?"

"We found it, all right," Danny said, "but we came almost losing it. They—"

"But you didn't?" Briton asked, breaking in roughly.

"No," Aunt Mabel said, "it isn't lost. I put it away for safekeeping."

The archaeologist sighed. "That's the best news I've heard for a month. We know just enough about it to keep us tantalized."

Aunt Mabel went into the bedroom. When she came back her face was ashen and her eyes staring.

"What's the matter?" Danny gasped.

"I-I've got the book," she said weakly, "but not the translation. It's gone. Gone!"

CHAPTER 12

SPIES IN THE JUNGLE

Silence hung heavily over the little room. Ron opened his lips as though to speak, but the words did not come out.

Finally Danny said, "Are you sure it's gone, Aunt Mabel? You hid the book. Maybe you hid your translation too."

She shook her head. "It was inside an old clock. I put it there only two hours ago." The life was out of her voice. "No, it's gone, all right."

Howard Briton was staring at her. "Did I understand you to say that you had translated that book?" he demanded. "One chap who had been a Latin student for forty years said he wouldn't even undertake the job."

"I wasn't able to translate too much of it," Aunt Mabel answered. "About a chapter and a half. Then I gave it up. It's so hard I don't know how anyone could translate it."

The archaeologist hesitated a moment, his forehead furrowing. "Was there anything important in what you did translate?" he asked her. "Anything that might help the people who stole it?"

"When I first began, I was afraid the whole job would be too difficult for me," she answered, "so I just scanned it until I found words which referred to an old city, or buildings, or that sort of thing. I'm afraid I might have translated the most important part of the whole book."

He walked over to the table, thoughtfully, and turned. "That does make it bad," he said. "Of course, we won't know whether you've translated the most important portions until we get an expert who can decipher all of it."

"But we found the old city!" Ron broke in. "We followed the directions Aunt Mabel gave us and finally found it this afternoon."

"Of course," Newton put in importantly, "I assisted Miss Orlis in the translation. On the difficult portions, that is. Had I had more time I could have done the rest of it."

But nobody was listening to him.

Briton turned to face Ron, his eyes widening.

"Now that is something!" he exclaimed to no one in particular. "First you found the book after we took such pains to hide it. Now you've translated a portion of it and have found an ancient city it describes."

"I guess we've messed things up for sure," Danny answered.

"On the contrary," Briton smiled. "I'm just admiring your ingenuity." He sat down beside the table and leaned forward, lowering his voice. "Tell me about that city. What's it like?"

He listened, enthralled, while Ron and the others broke in on one another excitedly in their haste to describe what they had found. When they finally finished Briton stood again.

"That's a sight I've got to see!" With that he turned to Aunt Mabel. "Did you translate anything about a sacred well or cave?" he asked. "These other finds are important all right, but the real prize would be the sacred well or cave."

"Why?" Ron asked, breaking in before Aunt Mabel could speak. "What's so important about that?"

"We aren't just sure that it would be such a prize," Briton replied. "I should have said that we think it would be." As he began to talk, he got up again, nervously. "We know that the Mayan people had a religion which demanded human sacrifices from time to time. And at the same time as they offered the young women as sacrifices to their gods they threw in gold and silver objects, jade, household utensils, and jewelry. Tradition and what we have been able to learn by translating some of their writings tell us that. If we could actually find a well or cave that has been used for that purpose we would be able to unravel much of the mystery which surrounds these people, as well as secure a priceless collection of artifacts."

Kay's lips were trembling. "Do you mean they actually killed young girls as a part of their religion?" she asked incredulously.

He nodded. "Horrible thought, isn't it?" He smiled a little crookedly. "I'd say it is fortunate for you that you weren't born back in those days. You're just about the age the priests used to sacrifice."

She shuddered. "If there had just been someone to have brought the Gospel of the Lord Jesus to them," she almost whispered. "It's so terrible to think of people living in such darkness and sin."

For the space of a minute conversation ceased.

"You might have something at that," Briton said, frowning thoughtfully.

"You asked me about any reference to a cave or well," Aunt Mabel said. "I was just coming to it. The book described a cave, and some of the things you've just told us, but it didn't say anything about the location of it, at least in the portion I translated."

"Hmm." He clicked his tongue against the roof of his mouth. "That changes things considerably. I'm going to have to take a calculated risk, assuming that the thieves won't be able to find that cave before I get the manuscript translated. With the description of the city given so clearly, the chances are very good that the sacred cave will be pinpointed too."

He took the book from the table and reached for his hat.

"I'm going to take this back to Mexico City," he said. "There's a scholar there who can master it quicker than anyone else. I'll be back as soon as he finishes the translation. Until then we'll just have to keep our fingers crossed."

"Is there anything we can do to help?" Danny asked. "I feel terrible that we've fouled things up for you the way we have."

"You've probably done as much with this as I could have done," Briton answered. "So don't feel bad."

"Is there anything we can do to help?" Ron repeated.

The archaeologist smiled. "Maybe you can go over and find the cave for me," he laughed. "Then all I'll have to do is come and gather up the treasure."

The others laughed, but Newton Jonathan Edward Bostwick III was dead serious. "We shall endeavor to do as you suggest," he said. "When we find the cave would you prefer to have us transport the valuables to a place of safekeeping, or would you rather catalog them in the precise location where we find them?"

Briton was taken aback. "Well, I'll tell you, Sherlock Holmes," he answered momentarily, "if you discover the treasure perhaps you had better leave it where you find it. And I'd especially want you to leave the skulls where they are. If you should fall down with an armload of them, you might break some."

Ron saw the twinkle in Briton's eyes and smiled, but Newton shivered. "I-I think I shall l-l-leave all of it right w-w-where it is," he stammered.

When the archaeologist left, Danny walked over and closed the door behind him. Then he turned slowly.

"Well," he said, "what do you make of that?"

"You know," Ron answered, "I was just thinking, if there is a cave over there it shouldn't be so hard to find. The ancient city is quite flat. In fact, I can only remember that one hill, the one that big building was on. And a cave would have to be in a side hill."

"Most of them are, I guess," his brother answered.

"But not all of them," Newton countered. "I have read certain references to caves which were in perfectly flat country."

"It's worth a try to find it, anyway."

Before getting ready for bed that evening Ron got his Bible and brought it into the living room. Newton squirmed a little, uncomfortably.

"I think I'll be turning in," he said lamely.

Kay looked up at him appealingly. "Won't you wait for devotions, Newton?" she asked. "It will only take a few minutes."

Reluctantly he sat down again.

Ron opened the Bible and began to read from the tenth chapter of the Book of John.

"I am the door; if anyone enters through Me, he will be saved, and will go in and out and find pasture."

Ron paused significantly when he had finished

that verse. For a brief instant, his eyes met Newton's. They spoke to one another, wordlessly.

"It's the only way anyone may be saved," he said at last. "It's the only way any of us can have eternal life."

"That's one man's opinion," Newton protested, his cheeks flaming.

"That's the Bible's edict," Ron corrected him. "And the Bible is the Word of God."

He didn't press the subject further, as he saw Newton's temper rising, but later, when he was in the darkness of their room, Ron prayed silently, earnestly, for his friend.

The following morning, they were all up shortly after daylight, and prepared to go back to the ancient city.

"I wish we could go with you," Christine said as they left the house after breakfast. "But the Indian woman we went to take care of is still very ill. We'll have to go over and see her again."

"Don't worry," Ron laughed, "we'll tell you all about it when we get back tonight."

"If we get back," Miguel Hidalgo corrected ominously.

"Miguel!" Kay exclaimed. "Don't say things like that."

"It not good to go back there," the Indian boy repeated. "The evil spirits, they not like." He shook his head. "Much bad."

Nevertheless, when the others had crawled into the station wagon, Miguel got in after them.

For some reason it didn't seem to take nearly as long to get to the place where they had always left the station wagon and entered the jungle on foot. The boys intended to leave it on the road as they had the day before, but Kay protested.

"If those two men come along and happen to see it," she said, "they'll know we're here. And now that they've got the directions to help them locate the city they could be here."

"I'd never thought of that," Danny answered.

"Why don't you pull it off the road over there?" Ron asked, pointing to a narrow slit among the trees. "We could cover it with vines, and brush out the tracks, and they'll never know it's there."

"Best idea you've had for a month," Danny told him.

"I think of things like that all the time," Ron replied. "The only trouble is you don't recognize how good some other ideas have been."

When they had the station wagon completely hidden, they began to retrace their steps of the day before.

"You know," Ron exclaimed, wiping his moist forehead half an hour or so later, "I think this jungle has gotten thicker just since yesterday."

"Maybe old Bushy Eyebrows and our fake Mr. Briton will get into this stuff and decide they don't want to find the old city after all," Danny observed.

"Such imaginings could correctly be called wishful thinking," Newton warned him. "Those individuals impressed me as being desperate enough to endure any hardships in order to obtain their goal."

"Those are big words, Newt," Ron said, shaking his head. "Don't you ever get tired of lugging them around with you?"

Miguel, who had been silent since they left the road and had made their way down the steep incline and into the swamp, stopped suddenly. His hand went up in warning.

"What is it?" Kay asked, her voice catching suddenly. She was standing where she could see the spasm of fear that flashed across the boy's face.

Miguel shook his head and placed a warning finger upon his lips.

"Someone coming," he hissed. "They come—real close!"

Ron and his companions froze where they were and glanced wildly about.

"Who do you think it is?" Ron demanded under his breath.

Miguel motioned to them, silently, to follow him off the little game trail they had been following, to an opaque screen of vines and brush. "Stay here," he whispered, the words scarcely audible, "and keep quiet."

Ron looked over at Kay. She had bowed her head. Danny was praying too.

"O heavenly Father," Ron began to pray silently, "be with us and help these men to go on."

At first Ron, crouching tensely in the swamp, could hear nothing. But Miguel's ears were attuned to the jungle. And in half a minute or so Ron heard them, faintly at first, and then louder, as they came crashing noisily through the jungle. The color fled from his cheeks and his hands began to tremble.

"It must be those kids we've been following," the one who had posed as Howard Briton said as they came within earshot. "They're the only other ones who would know anything about that old city, and where it's supposed to be located."

"Let's hope you're right, Bart," Joe retorted. "If the real Howard Briton gets his mitts on you, it'll be too bad."

"Listen," Bart snapped, his voice tinged with anger. "You're in this thing just as deeply as I am. And when we find all that gold, silver, and jade that's supposed to be in that cave you'll be after your share of it."

Ron's body stiffened. So, Bart and Joe were the ones who had stolen the translation. And when they find the city, they'd know as much as Ron and his companions did!

And then, without warning, Ron sneezed. A loud, unmistakable sneeze! It came so suddenly he didn't even have an opportunity to muffle it with his hand! Fear charged through his veins, stiffening him instantly. Kay gasped, and Miguel's dark eyes filled with terror!

"What was that?" Joe cried.

The two men must have been standing motionless. A grim, breathless silence seemed to envelop them.

"Those kids!" his companion exclaimed. "They're here!"

CHAPTER 13

LOST IN THE JUNGLE

For a long, agonizing moment Ron and his companions crouched in the murky, stagnant swamp. Bart and Joe had taken four or five steps toward them, and had stopped again, listening. Ron chewed on his lower lip nervously and crouched even lower, as though trying to get the swamp to swallow him. Newton, who was standing beside him, had grasped his arm, convulsively, and squeezed until Ron's arm ached.

"They're over there!" Bart cried after an instant or two. "We've got to get them or they'll ruin everything!"

"I'll pulverize them!" Joe snarled. "That's what I'll do!" They crashed forward again, three or four steps, and stopped. Ron couldn't see them, but he knew they were straining to see through the curtain of green, trying to catch a glimpse of him, or one of the others.

"They're going to get us!" Newton whispered in Ron's ear. "I just know they are!"

Miguel's hand went up and his flashing eyes warned Newton to silence.

"I can't see a thing in this blasted jungle!" Joe snapped. And then the sneeze came back.

Ron felt it coming, a faint, impulsive tickling in his nose. He caught his breath and threw both hands to his nose and mouth. But he was too late! The sneeze came out, distorted and muffled. But it was a sneeze.

Bart shouted triumphantly. "They're over here, Joe! Come on! Let's get 'em!"

"Quick!" Danny shouted. He grasped Kay by the arm and started to run at top speed through the jungle. "This way!"

Ron and Newton, who had been four or five paces ahead of the others, turned and almost stumbling over one another in their haste, tried to follow. But Bart saw them.

"Stop!" the pseudo archaeologist shouted loudly. "Stop, or I'll shoot!"

Ron's heart had come up into his throat and was throbbing there, convulsively. Great pearls of sweat had oozed out onto his forehead and trickled down his grime-stained face as he burst into a weird, spread-legged run.

Newton, who was half a step behind him, was breathing in great, tearing gasps.

The boys threw themselves over the tangle of ferns and roots and clumps of rough ground which dotted the murky ooze like cobblestones set too far apart.

"Stop!" Bart ordered.

The boys were running as fast as they could, but the wiry little man was gaining on them. They could hear him crashing through the brush and dead timber, as he drew closer and closer.

"And you'll be sorry you tried to get away from us when I do get my hands on you!"

Ron cast a quick, desperate glance over at Newton. The boy's eyes were wide with terror and his cheeks were puffed like a chipmunk's. Ron's own legs were throbbing with fatigue. He could scarcely run another step. But he had to! They dare not stop now!

At that instant it happened. There was a crashing noise behind him, and a scream of terror!

"Snake!" Bart screamed. "Snake! It's going to kill me, Joe! It'll kill me!"

The suddenness of his cry stopped the boys for a split instant.

"What's the matter with you?" Joe demanded roughly.

"Kill it, Joe!" Bart pleaded. "It's got me by the foot! Kill it!"

"What's the matter with you?" Joe demanded, disgust in his voice. "All you did was catch your toe in a vine!"

"Are-are you sure?"

"Come on, get up before I lose my temper!" Joe ordered. "Can't you tell the difference between a twig and a snake? Another hundred yards and we'd have had those blasted kids!"

By that time Ron and Newt had begun to creep to one side, stealthily, making their way in silence over the roots, as they had watched Miguel do.

"If they get away, Bart Davis, I'm going to hold you responsible! I don't know why I let you in on this deal. You always bungle everything."

"Whose deal was this, anyway?" Bart asked, plaintively. "Besides, those kids can't be too far away!"

The silence was deafening. Ron and Newton paused, crouching among the fern, every muscle tense and motionless.

"There's no use trying to hunt for them anymore," Joe retorted, his voice thick with disgust. "Come on. Let's see if we can find that city. Maybe you haven't ruined that for us."

For two or three minutes Ron and Newton could hear the two men walking noisily back to the trail. They were arguing again, but without enthusiasm. Finally, they were out of hearing.

"Well," Newton sighed, straightening, "they're gone."

Ron nodded. "But there's no telling when they'll be back," he said softly.

"W-w-what do you think we should do?" his companion asked.

"We'd better wait here. If we go to floundering through the jungle until Bart and Joe have had time to get quite a way from us, we might stumble onto them again."

Five minutes passed, and then ten. There was no sound in the jungle except the chatter of the monkeys, and the cry of innumerable parrots from somewhere in the swamp.

"I think we should be able to go on now," Ron said at last.

Newton looked about, bewilderedly. "Which way should we go?"

Ron did not answer him. Instead, he took a step or two forward, uncertainly, and looked about.

"I wish I knew which direction Danny and the others went," he said. "We should find them if we can."

"Danny," Newton called loudly.

"Don't do that," Ron cried, clapping his hand over the boy's mouth. "You'll have Bart and Joe on our necks for sure."

Newton was terrified. "But we've got to do something," he said, his mouth quivering.

"The worst thing we can do is get scared," Ron said. "You know, we live in some desolate country on the Angle. Dad always says that panic kills more men than the wilderness does. Just take it easy, Newt. It won't help any to get excited!"

"But we're lost!"

"We'll find our way," Ron replied with a firmness he did not feel. "We got in here. We'll get out. Don't worry about that."

"It's all right for you to talk that way," his companion retorted; "if anything happens to you, you're all right."

For an instant Ron did not understand what he meant. A question came into his eyes.

"I mean you'll be-be taken care of if you die!"

"You can be taken care of, too, Newton," Ron told him earnestly. "All you have to do is to confess that you are a sinner, need a Savior, and put your trust in the Lord Jesus for salvation."

Newton swallowed hard, but for the space of two or three minutes he said nothing.

"It-it doesn't seem right, somehow, that it's as easy as that," he said at last. "It seems to me that a fellow should have to do a little something to earn it."

Ron pursed his lips. "I'll see if I can explain it," he began. "If you were in the tallest building back home in Minneapolis, and wanted to get a ride to the top, would you get on the elevator on the ground floor or walk up to the sixth?"

"That's a stupid question. Anybody would get on the elevator on the ground floor. A fellow could hardly walk to the top of the tallest building anyway. It would be silly to walk partway."

"That's exactly the way it is with salvation," Ron answered. "Only you *could* walk to the top of the tallest building if you had the strength and wanted to walk long enough. But you couldn't get to Heaven by being good. The Bible tells us that even the best of us couldn't be nearly good enough to be worthy of Heaven. That's why salvation is provided as a free gift. All you have to do is confess that you are a sinner, need salvation, and put your trust in Jesus to save you. But," he paused significantly, "you've got to mean business."

"Those verses you've been reading to me," Newton continued, "I haven't been able to get them out of my mind. Guess I hardly slept at all last night. And now—" His voice died away.

"You know, Newt," Ron said, "you'll never really be happy until you do confess your sins and take Jesus as your Savior."

Together they bowed their heads and Newton Bostwick began to pray. His prayer was halting, but from the depths of his heart. When he finished, Ron prayed for him, also that God would help them to find their way back to the little village.

* * *

Danny and Kay and their Indian guide, Miguel, crashed noisily through the jungle the instant Bart and Joe began to run toward them. For several minutes they scrambled over fallen trees and roots and pushed excitedly through the jungle and swamp. The sweat stood out on their arms and foreheads, and their whole beings tingled with exhaustion.

"I've got to stop and rest, Danny," Kay gasped at last, faltering. "I just can't go on anymore."

"We've got to!" he ordered sternly. "We can't let them catch us!" With that he reached back and grasped her by the hand, pulling her after him.

How long they labored through the vast jungle they did not know. Time ceased to exist, and space became a nightmare of swamp water and trees and crawling things. At last Danny stopped. His shoulders sagged, and his breath tore savagely at his lungs. For almost a minute they did not speak. Then Kay looked about.

"Where're Ron and Newton?"

"They were right behind us."

"They get them," Miguel announced with conviction. "I tell you about evil spirits. They get—"

"I'm sure they would be able to get away," Kay said hopefully. "They could outrun those two men."

Danny was silent.

"It might be as well," he said softly, "if Bart and Joe had gotten them. At least they wouldn't be lost in this jungle!" Terror filled Kay's eyes.

* * *

Ronald Orlis continued to move forward steadily, and Newton stayed almost at his elbow.

"The important thing," Ron said, "is for us to go in a straight line. Most fellows, when they are lost, go in a big circle."

"You know, Ron," Newton said, "I may be a Christian now, but I don't feel anything is different."

"One of our neighbors up on the Angle became naturalized last summer," Ron answered. "I heard Dad ask him if he felt different. Mr. Olson said he couldn't say that he did, but as far as Uncle Sam was concerned, he was different. As far as God is concerned, you're different too. You don't have to worry. The feeling will come as you begin to live the way Jesus wants you to live."

Ron wasn't sure how long they had been tramping through the swamp, but he knew that they should have reached the road by this time. They had left the swamp twenty minutes before and had been climbing steadily ever since. It had taken less than five minutes to reach the road from the swamp the day before.

"What's the matter, Ron?" Newton asked tensely, as the boy paused. "Is there something wrong?"

"I don't know," Ron answered. "I thought we were heading toward the road, but I must have fouled up some place."

At the top of the ridge Newton grasped his arm tightly.

"Look!" There before them lay the ancient city.

"What do you know!" Ron exclaimed. "We went in exactly the opposite direction. And I was going to show you what a wonderful woodsman I am."

"That, most assuredly, does not annoy me," Newton said, smiling. "At least we know where we are now. We can find the old path, the one we took yesterday."

"I guess you're right at that." Ron stepped out into the little clearing and squinted up at the sky.

"It's still early in the afternoon," he said. "We've got plenty of time to get out of the jungle before dark. That's one good thing."

Newton was standing to one side, staring intently at first one half-standing wall, and then another.

"I can almost imagine what this city was like," he said at last, "back in those days when the people lived here. That building over there was probably one in which their rulers lived, and those ruins which look like big houses were probably the homes of the more wealthy people."

"What about that big one in the center?" Ron asked him. "The one on the hill?"

"That must be the temple," Newton answered. "Of course, it would be. Their religion was the center of their lives. Why wouldn't they make the temple in the center of their city?"

Ron took a deep breath.

"Now, if we could just find that sacred cave," he said.

Newton thought for a moment. "It might be close to the temple. In fact, it probably would be—especially with the temple on a hill. The cave could be somewhere below it." His voice rose excitedly. "Come on! Let's take a quick trip around that hill before we start back."

Together they walked rapidly around the hill, looking up at the tumbled ruins and at the steep slopes which dropped away from the ancient building.

They must have spent two hours or more walking around the hill and exploring the steep sides. Finally, they stopped at the base of the hill and looked up toward the wide, glistening white steps which led up to what must have been the front of the temple. The sun was lower now, and long, eerie shadows were cast about the ruins. Newton grasped Ron's shoulder suddenly.

"Look up there!" he cried. "Do you see the outline of that path winding down from the steps?"

Ron shook his head.

"Look in the shadows," his companion told him. "See, the trees and undergrowth are considerably lower, in a long, narrow, winding strip."

Ron nodded. "I see it."

"That path could lead to the cave!" Newton continued.

"Do you—" But Ron didn't get to finish.

"There they are!" a hoarse voice shouted loudly from somewhere behind them.

They whirled to see Bart and Joe standing beside a tall granite column some two hundred yards away!

"You're not going to get away this time!"

CHAPTER 14

RESCUED!

For a time, it seemed as though neither Ron nor Newton could move. They stood there, staring stupidly back at Bart and Joe.

"All right, you two!" Joe shouted so loudly that his voice reverberated through the silent jungle. "If you know what's good for you, you'll stay where you are!"

The anger in his voice sent spears of ice stinging into Ron's heart.

"You can't get away this time!" The two men burst into top speed, scrambling over the huge granite blocks toward Newton and Ron. "Don't move!" Bart shouted. "It'll be too bad for you if you do!"

"Come on, Newt!" Ron exclaimed, suddenly finding strength in his legs. "We can't let them get us!"

The boys whirled and began to scramble up the steep hill.

Joe cursed and shouted at them again.

"Don't pay any attention to him," Ron panted.

"Where are we going?" his companion wasted precious breath to ask.

Ron shook his head. A prayer came, unspoken, to his heart.

By this time, they had managed to put a screen of trees between them and the two men who were scrambling desperately toward them.

"Let's head for that path!" Newton suggested. "It's our only chance!"

Bart and Joe were drawing closer now. They weren't wasting any time or breath in talking but climbed up the hill as fast as they could.

"We've given them the slip again," Newt whispered.

Ron shook his head. "They'll be back. This time they know we can't get off this hill. We're sunk, Newt."

Newton got silently to his feet. "I have an idea," he whispered.

With great stealth he inched up to the place where the trees were shorter.

"Look at this, Ron," he said, scarcely mouthing the words. "You can see exactly where the path is once you get up here."

The young boy nodded, the beat of his heart quickening. The footsteps of countless thousands during past centuries had worn a deep, narrow winding path around the hill. It was simple to follow, as simple as though it were paved and marked with yellow signs.

"Do—do you think we can find the cave?" he whispered.

Newton nodded. "We'll have to pray that we will."

Quickly, but as silently as possible, they moved along the path, their eyes searching the steep bank to their left as they walked along.

Bart and Joe were above them now. Ron could hear their footsteps, their violent cursing.

"They're up here somewhere!" Joe snapped bitterly. "They've got to be!"

Ron felt the goose bumps come out on his neck. If Bart and Joe got them now there was no telling what would happen! He quickened his pace subconsciously. Newton did the same. They had moved scarcely two hundred yards when Ron saw it! There was a small dark hole, hidden at the back of a thick drapery of vines!

"Over here, Newt!" he exclaimed under his breath.

Diving off the trail he pushed aside the vines, and there it was! A thin, narrow slit between two giant boulders!

"We've found it! We've found it!"

"Hurry up and get in there!" Newton ordered, shoving him. "Those guys are right behind us!"

Ron dove inside, and Newton followed him.

* * *

When Danny and Kay and the Indian boy drove back to the mission station and told the missionaries what had happened, Aunt Mabel turned quickly to the native guide.

"Miguel," she ordered crisply, "go tell your father what has happened. Tell him to get as many men together as he can. We'll have to get back over there and hunt for the boys. We've got to find them before nightfall."

Kay's small face was white and drawn. And a tear, that had been glistening in her eye, slipped its mooring and began to trickle slowly down her cheek.

"Danny," she began softly, "I don't know what we'll do if-if we don't find Ron and Newton."

"We'll have to put our trust in the Lord Jesus that we will find them," he answered.

"I can't help feeling that it's our fault," she continued. "We should have stayed there. We should have waited for them."

Danny shook his head. "That wouldn't have done any good. Besides, Ron's able to take care of himself."

"I wish I could be sure of that."

"I am concerned about them, Kay," Danny said; "I've got to admit that. But we know the Lord Jesus can take care of them. We'll just have to do the best we can and put our trust in Him."

She nodded, smiling.

"You'd better wipe away those tears," he told her gently. "Here come Juan Hidalgo and some of the Indian men."

Miguel and his dad and six or eight others came crowding about the front door.

"We go," Juan said simply.

"Oh, that's wonderful," Christine answered.

"Where is this place that the Americano is lost?" the Christian Indian asked.

It was Miguel who answered, his voice quivering. "Over by the place where the two rivers meet," he said. "The place where nobody goes!"

Juan blanched a little and turned to his companions to translate. There was a chorus of excited jabbering. Juan began to gesture wildly, his voice rising as he talked. But it was of no use! One by one the men turned deliberately and stalked away.

"What's the matter?" Christine asked. "What's wrong?"

Juan Hidalgo turned to her sorrowfully. "Nobody ever go over where the two rivers meet," he said. "Our fathers, nor our fathers' fathers, for as long as our people have been here. Evil spirits there, they say. Much hurt. They no go."

"Can't you convince them?" she asked him desperately. "Did you tell them about the boys?"

He nodded miserably. "They not go."

Chris turned miserably to her missionary companion. "What are we going to do, Mabel?"

Juan Hidalgo drew himself up with grim determination. "Miguel and me," he announced, "we go."

Miguel swallowed hard.

* * *

Ron Orlis and Newton Bostwick crouched tensely in the mouth of the cave. They could hear Bart and Joe laboring up the steep slope.

"O heavenly Father," Ron prayed silently, "just keep them from finding us!"

"I don't know what could have happened to them!" Joe snapped from a spot not twenty yards away from the cave where they were hiding.

"At least you can't blame it on me because they got away this time."

"They're on this hill," Joe continued. "We know that much. They won't be able to get away without us seeing them."

"You go one way," the pseudo archaeologist ordered, "and I'll go the other. We can't let them get away this time!"

Inside the cave Ron shifted slowly. His foot touched something round and smooth. It moved a little and he jumped, startled.

"What's wrong now?" Newt whispered in his ear.

"My foot touched something. It scared me for a minute."

By this time, their eyes had become accustomed to the darkness.

"Look at the way those stones are piled," Ron said presently. "The little one's on the bottom and all the others are resting on it. See, they all move when I give this one a little push!"

"Look out!" Newton retorted, grasping Ron's foot with both hands. "Don't do that or we'll be locked in here for good! Whoever placed those here fixed them so that if the little one was kicked out of the way all the others would fall, blocking the entrance."

Ron looked at the stones carefully. Newton was right. They had been set up, one against the others, like so many dominoes; arranged so that when the smallest was kicked out, the others would fall in turn, completely blocking the cave entrance!

"Man! That's a nice little contraption for suicide!" Instinctively Ron drew away from the stones.

"That means something though, Ronald," Newton said, studying the rocks carefully. "That means this is no ordinary cave."

"Do you suppose it could be the sacred cave?"

"A true scientist never ventures a guess until the evidence is overwhelming," Newton said, "but I am confident that we have discovered the sacred cave of Zongolica!"

He stooped over and picked up a broken piece of jade, and a small piece of pottery.

"The ancient Mayans had the idea that objects which they made had life," he said. "Therefore, when they performed their human sacrifices they always 'killed' a few pieces of jewelry and some cooking utensils, or gold ornaments, along with their sacrificial offerings."

Ron would have ventured farther back into the cave, but Newton stopped him. "If those pagan priests fixed up a booby trap like this to close off the entrance to this cave," he said, "there's no knowing what they've got rigged out farther back. We'd better wait until we get Danny here and a good electric lantern."

Ron shook his head admiringly. "I've got to hand it to you, Red," he said. "You think of just about everything."

Newton did not reply. Three minutes passed, and then four.

"I'm sorry about calling you Red, Newton," Ron apologized at last. "I didn't mean to make you mad."

"You didn't," his companion answered. "The fact is, even though I acted like it made me decidedly angry, I rather enjoyed it. Rather distinctive name, don't you think?"

Ron looked at him crookedly and grinned.

Finally, when the boys were sure that Bart and Joe had gone, they stole out of the cave and went down the steep hillside.

"Now," Ron said, still whispering, "if we can just get back to the village, and get Danny and the others, and get back here before those two find the cave."

"Maybe we should go back and camouflage it a little better," Newton said. "Since we found it the way it is, they just might find it, too."

They went back to the cave and, taking vines, covered the mouth of it so perfectly it couldn't be seen ten feet away.

"There, Red," Ron said when they had finished. "Now we won't need to worry about them finding it."

"All we've got to worry about now," his companion said, "is that twenty or twenty-five-mile walk back home."

Ron groaned. "You think of the most pleasant things!"

The sun was going down and the jungle was growing dark when they finally made their way out of the swamp and up on the road.

"Now if we only had that station wagon!"

"Step to the phone and call Danny, Ron," Newton laughed. "Tell him to drive over and pick us up."

Even as he spoke a pair of headlights were switched on about thirty or forty yards ahead of them, bathing them in light.

"Bart and Joe!" Ron cried.

And then they heard Kay.

"Ron!" she squealed. "Oh, Ron!"

"It's Kay!"

By that time, she had jumped out of the station wagon, dashed up to him and threw her arms around him. He saw her coming and struggled to get away, but she smothered him in her arms and hugged him the way his mother would have done.

"What's the big idea?" Ron sputtered. "I'm not Danny! Let go of me! For cryin' out loud!"

In an instant she released him. "Oh, I'm so glad to see you, Ron!" she exclaimed again. "We gave up finding you once and came back to the station wagon when Danny and Juan decided they should make one more try. I've been sitting here praying—and thinking of all sorts of things that could have happened to you and Newton."

Ron eyed her critically and put the distance of another step between them. "If I'd known what was going to happen to me," he said, "I'd have stayed lost!"

CHAPTER 15

LOCKED IN THE CAVE

In a few minutes Danny and the others came dejectedly out of the jungle and headed toward the station wagon.

"We've just got to have help, Aunt Mabel," he said, opening the door. "We've got to have lots of help or we are never going to—" He stopped as he saw his brother sitting in the rear seat. "Ron!" he cried.

"N-n-now take it easy," Ron stammered, shrinking away from him. "I've been welcomed once!"

"Where have you been? What happened to you?"

Ron started to tell them what had happened, but Newton broke in dramatically.

"Daniel," he announced, clearing his throat importantly. "You are now resting your exhausted optics upon two extremely successful archaeologists, or should I say private investigators?"

"Whatever are you talking about, Newton?" Kay demanded. "What did you do? Why haven't you told us?"

His eyes were dancing, but his voice was serious. "You didn't ask us, Madam."

"Newton Bostwick," she stormed, "if you don't tell us, I'll—"

"Come on," Danny broke in impatiently. "Give."

With great deliberation Newton turned to Ron. "Shall I make our official statement?"

"You'd just as well shoot the works, Red."

"In that case, gentlemen and ladies, I wish to inform you that we accomplished that which we set out to do."

"You mean you found your way back here," Danny exclaimed disgustedly, "in only four or five hours more than it should have taken you."

"I mean, my dear fellow conspirator, that we have discovered the sacred cave of Zongolica! We have laid our hands upon the key which seems likely to be able to unlock the secrets of the past. At our very fingertips we have a treasure greater than that of the Incas. Today we have—" He stopped and stared significantly from one to the other.

A hush blanketed the little group. Danny's and Kay's eyes widened, and Aunt Mabel took hold of Christine's hand and squeezed it hard.

"You-you don't mean it!" Danny said, dully.

Newton paused until they were all leaning forward breathlessly. "Well," he said carelessly, "let us say that we found a cave."

"Newton Bostwick," Danny said ominously, "I've a good notion to—"

"Just call him Red," Ron cut in.

Danny turned to his brother. "That's about enough out of you. Come on, you guys, give! Or I'll have Juan cart both of you out into the jungle again, and this time we won't go looking for you."

"We did find a cave, Danny," Ron said seriously. "That's the truth."

"We don't know for sure whether it's the sacred cave or not," Newton continued, "but we did find a few pieces of pottery and a small object of jade. If we had a flashlight, we would have gone back into it a ways."

"Much bad," Miguel said brokenly. "Evil spirits guard cave, maybe. Very much bad. Better we hadn't go over there anymore."

"There were a couple of evil spirits back there," Ron said. "At least I *think* they were evil, but they weren't the kind you're thinking about, Miguel."

Danny looked at him questioningly.

Newton laughed.

"They should probably be described as exceedingly angry spirits," he explained. "They answered to the names of Bart and Joe, or as we knew the latter, 'Bushy Eyebrows.'"

Kay shuddered. "It gives me the cold chills just to think about them. You'll never know how glad I was to see you and Newton come out of the jungle."

Ron snorted. "I hope I never get lost around you again," he muttered. "I don't think I could stand it."

Kay laughed happily. "I don't think it was as bad as all that."

"You don't? I got two busted ribs and a cracked vertebra."

"That was because you struggled, my friend," Newton explained. "The moral of that is—"

"When you see Kay coming, *run!*" Ron finished cryptically.

"What's all this about?" Danny asked. "I'm about the only one who isn't in on this."

"I hesitate to tell you, Daniel," Newton answered. "I should not like to be the one to disillusion you about your brother and your girlfriend."

"They're just trying to tease me, Danny," Kay said, her cheeks flushing. "I was so glad to see Ron come out of the brush that I threw my arms around him. I guess it embarrassed him."

"Embarrassed nothing," Ron retorted. "It 'bout pulverized me."

"If that's all it is, Kay," Danny laughed, "you have my permission to hug him any time you want to."

Ron muttered something under his breath, but they couldn't hear it because of the laughter.

When they finally got back to the mission house, Ron and Newton took the pieces of pottery and the piece of jade out of their pockets as the others crowded around.

"I do believe you've found the sacred cave," Aunt Mabel said, turning the jade thoughtfully in her fingers. "There's no other explanation for finding these things in the mouth of the cavern."

"We should get over to the real Mr. Briton's camp," Danny said, "the first thing in the morning. We'll have to work fast, or Bart and Joe will find it too."

"Maybe we should go over tonight," Ron suggested.

Danny looked at his watch, and then toward Aunt Mabel and Christine.

"I think we should go to bed for two or three hours anyway," Chris answered. "It's a long way from the road to the city. We'll have to have some rest."

Ron thought he would never get to sleep that night, but finally he dozed off. And the next thing he knew Danny was shaking him roughly.

"Come on, fellow, we've got work to do."

Instantly he was awake.

"Red!" he called. "Red, come on! Hit the floor!"

Newton raised up on one elbow, sleepily rubbing at his eyes.

"Come on!" Ron said loudly. "We've got work to do!"

The boys picked up Miguel to guide them and drove over to the real Mr. Briton's archaeological camp. But he was not back from Mexico City yet.

Ron turned to Danny when Miguel had interpreted what the Indian had said. "What are we going to do?"

he asked. "We can't wait two or three days for Briton. Bart and Joe will have found the cave by that time!"

Danny's mouth drew down to a thin hard line. "Not if we get there first."

Back at the mission house Aunt Mabel and Kay decided that they wanted to go along.

"Miguel says it's much bad," Ron told them darkly.

"Oh, that doesn't bother us at all," Kay laughed. "You can't expect us to stay here when you've actually found the cave, Ron. Why, we'd just die of suspense waiting for you to come back."

They pulled away from the little village and drove as fast as they dared over the rough, twisting road to the place where they had to leave the station wagon.

"What I hope," Ron said, looking nervously about, "is that we don't come across those two guys."

"Evil spirits will be much angry," Miguel said uneasily.

Newton turned to the boy. "You shouldn't be worried about evil spirits, Miguel," he said, his voice strangely serious. "You should do as I did yesterday and put your trust in the Lord Jesus. Then you'd never have to worry about things like that again."

Miguel stared at him. "You?" he asked, incredulously. "But I thought—"

Danny, Kay, and Aunt Mabel had turned to face him too.

"Do you mean that, Newton?" Danny asked.

"Of course, I do," the boy replied. "I confessed my sins and put my trust in the Lord Jesus yesterday."

"That's wonderful," Kay breathed.

"It's more than that," Newton answered. "I don't know how I ever thought I could be happy without the Lord Jesus."

The Indian boy shook his head. "But you say there is nothing to this Bible business," he said to Newton. "You say Book not true. Salvation not mean anything."

"That was because I didn't like to have the Bible tell me that I was a sinner and in need of a Savior, Miguel," Newt went on. "But I know now that there's only one way to eternal life. There's only one way to be truly happy, and that's to do like the Bible says. Confess that you are a sinner and give your life to-to Christ."

Miguel hesitated. There were questions and deep concern in his eyes.

"No," he said doggedly. "No. It not for me."

Danny was watching him. "You think about it, Miguel. We'll all be praying for you."

For a brief instant, the Indian boy's face lighted up. "You pray that evil spirits no hurt Miguel?" he asked.

"We'll be praying that you take Jesus as your Savior," Danny answered.

Aunt Mabel took over, explaining to Miguel what Danny meant, using his native language. Still, he shook his head doggedly.

"No. No."

They went into the jungle and made their way laboriously through the swamp to the ancient city and the hill upon which the temple was set. At the entrance to the cave, they paused.

"I don't remember leaving it like this," Ron muttered.

"Neither do I," Newton put in. "We didn't have nearly so many vines covering the opening."

"Do you suppose Bart and Joe did find it, Red?"

"You guys were probably so scared and excited you didn't know what you were doing," Danny told them.

In a moment or two they had swept the vines away from the mouth of the cave and stepped into the inky blackness.

"Oh, Danny!" Kay gasped, pressing close to his side. "It-it's so dark in here."

In response he switched on the powerful electric lantern which he had brought along.

"Look!" Ron cried, pointing a trembling finger along the shaft of light.

The beam revealed ten or twelve feet of hard stone floor, and that was all. The shaft of light dropped off into space, to reflect eerily against the far end of the vaulted chamber which extended both above and below them like the lobby of some great hotel.

Cautiously they crept forward and looked down. It was almost a hundred feet to the smooth, stone floor of the cave below. For several minutes they stood there silently, while Danny swept the floor of the room below with the powerful light. There were broken pieces of pottery and stone scattered about the floor.

"What's that?" Kay asked, pointing.

There in one corner was a small pile of gold and silver dishes and small urns.

"Bart and Joe have been here!" Newton cried. "The priests would never have piled those things like that."

"M-m-maybe it was someone else," Kay stammered hopefully, "someone who came here centuries and centuries ago."

"It couldn't be," Ron answered. "Isn't that a glove, or a piece of dark cloth on the floor beside that pile?"

While they were staring down at the small object there was a sudden noise outside.

Danny switched off the light.

"Did-did you hear that?"

"They're coming!" Newton exclaimed.

"W-w-what are we going to do?"

"The spirits," Miguel said plaintively. "They—"

"Look out!" Newton ordered. With that he pushed past the others and ran to the pile of stones Ron had kicked slightly the day before.

"Don't!" Ron shouted in warning.

But it was too late. Newton had already given the small stone, which held the others precariously in place, a sharp kick. There was a resounding roar! The little cavern filled with dust! Then all was quiet.

"What did you do?" Kay and Aunt Mabel demanded, their voices quavering.

"I stopped them," Newton replied. "We won't have to worry about them getting in here now!"

Ron turned to face him. In spite of himself his face was white and drawn and his lower lip was trembling.

"No," he said unevenly, "they can't get in. But we can't get out either!"

CHAPTER 16

THE WAY OUT

It was a tense, frightened group that stood in the entrance of the cave, staring blankly into the darkness. The noise had ceased now. All was silent in the cave, except for their heavy breathing.

"What we do now?" Miguel demanded, his voice trembling. "What we do?"

For a long minute no one answered him.

"What are we going to do?" Kay echoed in a small, thin voice.

Danny turned on the light, bathing the cave entrance in its powerful beam. "That trap must have held thirty tons of rock in place," he said. "It's a certainty we won't be able to dig our way through that mess. Whoever rigged it up made mighty certain of that."

"It is the spirits," Miguel continued. "I tell you, we cannot disturb the spirits. Now we all be killed."

"I think we should talk to the Lord about it," Aunt Mabel suggested calmly. "We've had many times when our troubles looked so high and overwhelming that we couldn't see a way through them, but God showed us the way."

They all knelt together on the hard stone floor, in a tight little circle. Ron prayed first, softly, earnestly. When he had finished, Newton took his turn. He thanked God for his salvation, and then pleaded earnestly that the Lord would keep them and guide them to safety. The others prayed in turn. When Aunt Mabel had finished and they started to get to their feet, Miguel took hold of Ron's arm.

"Wait," he said tensely.

Ron turned to face him.

"If Miguel die," he began shakily, his voice thickening with accent in his concern. "If Miguel die, he no go to Heaven."

"Not unless you confess your sins and accept Christ as your Savior," Ron told him. "You'll have to do what the Bible says, Miguel, and put your trust in Jesus to save you and give you eternal life."

The silence lengthened.

"Miguel want to be like you," he choked at last. So much of his own language had come into his voice as he spoke that they could scarcely understand him.

As Ron guided him, he prayed, slowly, haltingly, the words coming out as though they were torn, one by one, from his lips.

The Indian boy stopped praying at last and looked up self-consciously. In the dim reflected light of the electric lantern Ron saw that Miguel's face was still white and drawn.

"Do you realize what you've done, Miguel?" Aunt Mabel asked him in his native language. And then she went over the plan of salvation again, from the very beginning.

"*Si*," he said, his face lighting up when she had finished. "*Si*, Miguel understand."

When they had all gotten to their feet Newton said, "A most comforting thought just occurred to me. If those priests fixed that trap at the mouth of the cave so that it could be blocked from the inside, they must have done it to protect themselves from enemies."

"I don't see how that can help us," Kay told him.

"They most assuredly would never have planned on blocking off that entrance," Newt continued, "unless they had some other means of getting out of this place."

"I believe you're right," Danny replied. "All we've got to do is hunt until we find it."

"Absolutely, Daniel. Absolutely."

"That's what I like about you, Red," Ron observed. "Nobody can understand you. Not even you."

Kay took the light and, stepping forward carefully, looked down the sheer stone cliff.

"But how are we going to get down there?" she asked. "They must have used wooden ladders, or vines, or something. And we don't have a thing!"

Danny and Ron moved up beside her and began to examine the cliff.

"What you look for?" Miguel asked.

"Sometimes they carve hand and footholds in stone cliffs like this," Danny explained.

"Why didn't you inform me that was what you were searching for?" Newton asked, grandiosely. "You will find them to your left, almost in the corner."

Danny flicked the light toward the left. "There they are!" he exclaimed. "But how did you—" he looked at Newton incredulously.

"Just one of my many accomplishments," Newton said. "You might say that I am somewhat clairvoyant—but confidentially I saw them a few minutes ago and didn't know what they were until you mentioned them."

Kay swallowed hard. "Do-do you mean we're going to have to climb down those?" she stammered. "All the way to the bottom?"

"We're fortunate to find them," Danny told her.

"You can say that again," Ron put in. "I was just beginning to wonder how long a fellow could live without anything to eat."

The hand and footholds were old and worn, but they were still deep enough to give firm footing. Danny went down first, and then Aunt Mabel and Kay. And finally, Ron began to descend.

It had looked simple enough watching the others, but now that he was actually on his way down, cold sweat beaded his forehead and the palms of his hands until he was sure his fingers could no longer grip the granite handholds.

"How are you coming?" Newton called down to him.

"Better get ready to catch me," Ron answered. "Have you got a mattress handy?"

Finally, his trembling feet touched the solid rock floor. "There," he gasped weakly. "The ground never did feel so good to me before."

"Come on," Danny said. "We've got to keep on the move. Bart and Joe might think of a second entrance too."

"You bring up the most pleasant things!" Ron mumbled.

Before they left the big room Danny went over to where the gold objects were piled and examined them under the light.

"Oh, look at this!" Kay cried, picking up a piece of the precious metal which still had a large, ruby-like stone in it.

"And this," Aunt Mabel said, selecting a small gold statue. "I suppose this is one of their gods. It's the only thing in the pile that isn't broken."

"What'll we do with these things?" Ron asked. "Shall we take some of them with us if we can, Danny?"

His brother shook his head. "They're as safe here as they would be anywhere," he said, "even with us. Besides, we don't want to weight ourselves down."

"I think we should get started," Aunt Mabel said. "It might take us longer to find that other opening than we think."

They began to walk, single file, down the narrow, natural corridor which led out of the huge room.

"The air is fresh in here," Danny said. "That means the other opening can't be too far away."

"It can't be too close to suit me," Kay answered softly.

The tunnel twisted torturously, narrowing until they could scarcely squeeze through, and then widening to rooms almost as large as the first. Every now and then they came across little piles of broken pottery, cooking utensils, and jade.

"This gives me the willies, Red," Ron whispered in his friend's ear. "What would we ever do if we met someone heading the other way?"

"A foolish supposition," Newton replied, laughing. "Outside of Bart and Joe, who undoubtedly got no farther than the first big room, no one has even been in this cave for several hundred years."

At that moment Danny stopped suddenly.

"Psst!"

"What's the matter?" Ron whispered tensely.

"Someone's coming! Don't you hear them?"

"But there couldn't be!" Newton protested. "Nobody knows about this cave but us!"

Before Danny could speak again, they all knew that there was someone in the tunnel ahead of them. Someone who was coming their way!

"What are we going to do?" Kay asked tensely.

Ron looked behind him, desperately, into the inky blackness. What chance would they have of getting away from the intruders who were coming toward them? They could never make it through those narrow stretches in time to get away. And even if they did, what would they do when they came to the cliff, and the entrance which was so completely blocked with rock?

"There isn't anything we can do," Danny told her, miserably.

"Let's rush 'em!" Ron suggested. "Turn our light out, and when they get here, we'll all pile into them!"

Danny had already switched off the electric lantern. The boys crouched expectantly.

"They might get us," Ron gritted, "but they'll know they've been in a fight before they do."

And then they were blinded with light!

"You!" a voice exclaimed. "I might have known!"

"M-Mr. Briton!" Ron stammered.

The brilliant, blinding shaft of light moved to one side.

"What are you doing here?" Danny asked him.

"I was about to ask you the same thing," the archaeologist answered.

Ron sighed deeply. "I don't care how you happened to be here," he said. "I'm just glad it's you instead of Bart and Joe."

"We took care of them this morning," Mr. Briton said. "I brought a police officer from Mexico City with me, and a warrant for their arrest. We nabbed them not far from the cave entrance, a couple of minutes before you tripped that rockslide, or whatever it was you used to block up that entrance so tightly."

Ron and Newton looked at one another and laughed. "Then it was you we heard out there."

"That's right. Thanks to a few notes your Aunt had left in the book, the translator in Mexico City was able to save several days' work and finished translating the last of the book about midnight. It not only told the exact location of the cave but gave the location of the temple entrance as well." He paused a moment and smiled. "So, when you blocked that entrance, we hurried back to the temple and came in this way. We thought perhaps Bart Davis and his companion had some more friends in here. But I might have known it was you. I suppose you've already found everything there is to find in here."

Newton shook his head.

"The thing we were the most happy to find in here was you, Mr. Briton," he said. "If my red hair is white when we get out of here, you'll know it happened when you switched that light on us."

* * *

It was early morning. Ron and Newton had just finished packing their bags and had set them outside the kitchen door. Danny got the station wagon out of the garage and parked it a few feet from the back of the house.

"I sort of hate to go home, don't you?" Ron asked. Newton nodded.

"I suppose we won't even recognize the place the next time we come back. Wasn't it swell of Mr. Briton and his partners to donate half of what the sale of those artifacts found in the well will bring? They had permission from the Mexican government to go over this area. They wouldn't have had to give the mission anything."

"I guess it's like he said," Ron went on. "If it hadn't been for the help the translator got from Aunt Mabel's notes, it could have taken him so long that Bart and Joe would have had the stuff and slipped back into the United States, and the university wouldn't have gotten any of it."

"That hospital's going to be a big thing for the people here."

"You can say that again. It's going to be a big thing for the mission too. People will come for medicine or surgery and have an opportunity to hear the Gospel. Aunt Mabel and Kay's mother are both thrilled about it."

They sat down at the kitchen table.

"Where's Danny?" Newton asked.

Ron jerked his head toward the living room. "He's in there saying goodbye to Kay."

"Does it take that long?"

"How you talk!" Ron exclaimed. "Why, you know they aren't going to see each other until they get back to the Bible Institute at Cedarton. And that's six whole weeks."

Danny and Kay came into the kitchen just then, hand in hand. She was smiling radiantly, and for some reason Danny seemed happy and a little embarrassed.

"Now what's the matter with you two?" Ron demanded suspiciously.

Kay looked up at Danny. "Shall we tell them?" she asked.

Ron frowned darkly.

"Danny and I have been talking about the future," Kay said at last.

"And we've decided to share it," Danny blurted.

"Yes, Ron," she said, her eyes sparkling, "Danny and I are going to be married—when we're out of Bible school, of course."

Newton and Ron shook their heads solemnly.

"Her mother will never let you get away with it, Danny," Ron said. "She won't let Kay throw her life away on a big, broken-down, lovesick—"

"Easy, boy," Danny cautioned, grinning self-consciously. "I've already talked with her about it. She doesn't have any objections."

Ron got to his feet and walked over to Newton.

"Red, old boy," he said, "do you suppose Danny will ever regain consciousness?"

Red looked at Ron Orlis and winked.

"Unquestionably, my friend! Unquestionably!"

THE DANNY ORLIS SERIES

The Danny Orlis series, by Bernard Palmer, delivers a blend of adventure, mystery, and suspense through various settings—from the Canadian wilderness to Guatemalan jungles. Danny Orlis, an adept outdoorsman, skilled athlete, and committed Christian, employs his quick thinking, calm bravery, and biblical solutions to confront everyday problems and hair-raising dangers. Early stories focus on Danny navigating school life, sports, and outdoor challenges, while in later books, Danny and his wife Kay provide wisdom and guidance to youngsters facing lifelike situations and challenges. Having sold over two million copies, this series has made Palmer a renowned author in Christian youth literature. Palmer is also the author of the Felicia Cartright series and various other series for Christian youth.

AVAILABLE FROM WWW.ANEKOPRESS.COM

www.ingramcontent.com/pod-product-compliance
Lightning Source LLC
Chambersburg PA
CBHW070654100726

47907CB00007B/2202